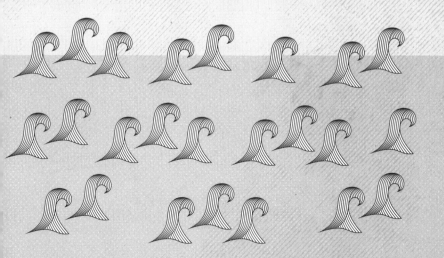

ARMY OF THE BRAVE AND ACCIDENTAL

Army *of the* Brave *and* Accidental

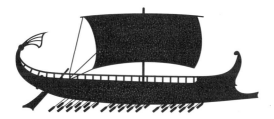

Alex Boyd

NIGHTWOOD EDITIONS | 2018

Copyright © Alex Boyd, 2018

ALL RIGHTS RESERVED. No part of this publication may be reproduced,
stored in a retrieval system or transmitted, in any form or by any means,
without prior permission of the publisher or, in the case of photocopying
or other reprographic copying, a licence from Access Copyright,
the Canadian Copyright Licensing Agency, www.accesscopyright.ca,
info@accesscopyright.ca.

Nightwood Editions
P.O. Box 1779
Gibsons, BC VON 1V0
Canada
www.nightwoodeditions.com

EDITOR: Amber McMillan
COVER DESIGN & TYPOGRAPHY: Carleton Wilson

Canada

 Canada Council   Conseil des Arts
for the Arts   du Canada

 BRITISH COLUMBIA
ARTS COUNCIL
An agency of the Province of British Columbia

Nightwood Editions acknowledges financial support from
the Government of Canada and the Canada Council for the Arts,
and from the Province of British Columbia through
the British Columbia Arts Council and the Book Publisher's Tax Credit.

This book has been produced on 100% post-consumer recycled,
ancient-forest-free paper, processed chlorine-free
and printed with vegetable-based dyes.

Printed and bound in Canada.

CIP data available from Library and Archives Canada.

ISBN 978-0-88971-341-3

for Elizabeth

Book One

1: Oliver

It happens that a man who'll be a murderer and the officer who'll arrest him walk down the same stretch of sidewalk together, years before they meet. Stories are larger than we think. Maybe there's only one story, and it's big. Falling back isn't a gentle float down a tunnel—it's closer to a packed bus on a summer day. It's suffocating and full of elbows. In some ways it was like travel on the sea. You could be pitched one way or another, in rougher or smoother patches, though it was an entirely translucent sea with all kinds of activity above and around you. They haven't perfected how to get the thick history of people out of the way and your bones want to unhook to get through it all. There's a kind of screaming you recognize and a kind of screaming you don't. You hear others complaining and unknown machinery creaking, and you catch glimpses of events turning and falling into place. A dictator learning to crawl.

I had yet to learn that I'd feel this many times over, skipping like a stone. Of course, it wasn't supposed to happen that way. I arrived and knew something was wrong right away. I took a few steps and fell over. I examined a tuft of grass and died. Not a literal death, but I was wrenched from that time like someone fighting to the surface and then pulled back under. There had been no way for me to know it would be like this. Is there a way for anyone to know? So with the first of my final moments I thought of Penelope, no bigger than a minute but strong. It changes your perspective on your remaining time when you've not only seen others die, you've died yourself once before. I thought of the email that I rediscovered months after Penelope sent it to me. She'd written out the song in her head as she waved goodbye before going to work that morning: "You are my sunshine, my only sunshine, you make me happy when skies are grey, you (something) know dear, how much I love you, please don't take my sunshine away." She was never good with remembering the words to a song. But it was that sunshine song in my head as I sailed again along thin rails of time, catching sight of a spinning moon.

My first morning with Penelope, we walked out on a summer day. She smiled at seeing a man on a patio who moved to give his waitress room to deliver a plate and put his arms straight up in the air, surrendering to his omelette. That's important to point out—she smiled and squeezed my hand, but she didn't laugh at him. I thought of her and saw this again, and again I saw her commenting on my round, handsome face, saying my dark hair was so short it made my ears stand out, like two seashells. She said, "You aren't the tallest or the craftiest man, but you're sturdy like an old stone building." In a blended landscape of moments I saw her generous smile and wheat-coloured hair. I saw her walking, comfortable in her own body. It was a body I used to hold at night and now I fell through the possibility it may be held by another.

I saw my childhood: it wasn't easy being a highly sensitive kid. Once, an older kid offered me a stick of gum and it was a trick—a bar snapped down on my finger like a mousetrap. I was so shocked a gesture of goodwill could be designed to humiliate me that I picked up a branch and hit the other kid with it while I looked up at him. I saw the fury in the eyes of the older kid, but my brother stood between him and me and talked him down. Upset, I threw open a wooden door in the basement so it hit the corner of the chest where my toys were kept. I could always put my finger in that splintered hole in the door and touch the mark my anger made, like a bullet hole. When another kid spat at me on the playground, the spittle came looping through the air and something hideous and inevitable made it land on the back of my coat. Competition makes you either withdraw or rise to meet it, and our world needs both types: one to keep things going, the other to think of better ways. I decided to compete only with myself.

Through the months of Penelope's pregnancy, I felt a low level of anxiety, as if I were on my way to the dentist for fillings. I'd read that first pregnancies are often delayed and prayed for a little extra time to watch old films and finish reading books. What if fatherhood wasn't for me? What if

I was a failure at the most important job in life? How was I to know I would like my son? There would be nothing to do but trudge through my duties, and I thought perhaps I could think back to some wave of experienced culture to draw from, given a little more time. And then began the shooting pains playing tag in my limbs, the shortness of breath. Long, anxious days of testing revealed it was inoperable, as though I wasn't meant to be a father, as though I'd taken a wrong turn.

Falling back in time you're like an idiot balloon. It's fairly expensive: there are those who argued it was ridding us of the greedy and the wealthy, though only after we'd allowed irretrievable damage to the planet. So there were two advantages: you could live out the rest of your life in a better world, and it was healing, your physical condition somehow reset. Don't ask me to explain it—I've spent my whole life using technology I can't explain. Naturally, there were long waits, but a cancellation and a rare opportunity opened up weeks before Tomas was only a month old.

And so I was folded up like a letter and sent back. They can only send people into the past. The rumour was that someone had gone into the future and simply dissolved into possibility. Only one echoing statement returned, saying he saw trucks sinking into the earth to rot like dinosaurs. I swam and pushed against the current but it was useless to do so. What would fatherhood mean to me now?

2: Oliver

"WE DON'T ALWAYS HAVE ANOTHER CHANCE TO GET it right, eh?" She only lifted her eyes from the page slowly, as though they had little weights on them. And yes, they use paper for the work they do when they send you. It's important that no information is lost, so first they inscribe it on paper that joyously soaks up ink, and then they type it into a database. You would think travelling through time would involve rows of blinking computer banks, like something out of an old film, or at least some kind of ceremony after all the press this had, but it was a woman with a notebook shoving me through a door. To be more accurate, an ornate metal framework door without walls, standing between you and the rest of the room. The woman was secured by a brace to avoid being caught up in the furious gusts of air that seem to want to fill the voids that have been created, and translucent images could be seen trading places and dying out on the far side of the room, beyond the door.

A piece of string secured at our end and running along the floor to the door frame suddenly lifted and toyed in the air around the centre of the frame like a needle in a gauge frantically trying to indicate something nobody could understand. She said, "Follow the piece of string but don't step beyond the point where it disappears—not yet." Turns out you can pull a string and unravel the world. She didn't even wear formal shoes and I tried not to look at her toes because they overlapped like a plate of sausages. It's a tough and competitive business, I told myself. I assumed she was also there because occasionally somebody needed a good shove.

That morning, I suddenly realized I'd reached the end of my natural life. I knew it was my last day in this life as I turned on the shower and lifted an arm, gesturing like a man in a showroom. What is it about humans that makes us note passing time but ignore the need to change anything? Youth is stubborn and invincible. Then we step behind the same set of eyes each day and fail to notice the first grey hairs, the slow change.

I arrived again, gasped and shook off the vague hands. Through a fence I could see a schoolyard corner where a few children had cornered another. The largest of them hit the cornered child with a stick and turned away. I took a step toward the lonely one that had been hit. For a second I thought I'd stepped in a pothole, but I hadn't—my body simply twisted and fell. Again, I would die where I arrived. What was happening? I needed a foothold, and to stay somewhere. It had better be different next time, I thought, looking at the child and closing my eyes.

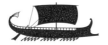

3: Penelope

WHEN WE MET, OLIVER AND I WERE LIKE A COUPLE of smoothly run countries at peace, discovering we bordered on each other. And I think that's quite rare, as there's so frequently a note of desperation on one side or another. "Are you participating in this thing too?" I turned to see his calm, steady eyes and the hint of a warm smile. We were both in the lobby of the Gladstone Hotel, where we'd been invited by a mutual friend to participate in a fundraiser for a theatre company. I liked the look of him and promptly shut him down completely. "Oh, yeah, but I need to talk to that guy over there," I said, walking away. It was true, I needed to rehearse a short skit I'd worked out with my friend, and Oliver had prepared a poem that was quite good for an amateur poet. A few hours later, the event over, we sat together in a small group where he was calm and perceptive.

I resent that I feel uncertainty now, and I'm not always sure where to direct the resentment. It's thinking of him without seeing him that gets me. There are ghosts creeping around in my peripheral vision, and some days he's everywhere. Whatever isn't him is something that fails to be him. When he first appeared, he was perfect: smart and calm, a beautiful smile. *Learn to be happy on your own*—such simple and impossible words after he left. I tried Internet dating; I phoned men while looking at my pathetically scrawled list of reasons why my husband was no longer the one for me, often carried in my pocket like a tiny shield against a storm. I couldn't even tell you what was on it, except for one note saying he was gone and would never come back.

Oliver said there was little point in being angry about anything. He said God was like an absent-minded person who keeps a lot of fish in an aquarium, and sometimes forgets to change the water or feed them, eventually noticing some of them have died. It isn't that God is against you, just that he sets things in motion and gets distracted. I could never tell him that after those first few dates, when we were finally and unabashedly looking into each other's eyes, I literally did thank God. I asked for a life with him and said I'd be extra kind and happy. Decent. And maybe God said, *Here's the real challenge: lose what you want most and figure out how to do that anyway.*

One man I phoned spoke slowly and told boring stories, so a few days before we were to meet I emailed him and said sorry, but someone had stepped on my heart. It wasn't recent news, but it was true. I met so many men through the Internet they began to blur together: they had a twin brother and were an only child, they were vegetarians and loved meat, they had backpacked everywhere and they'd never left home, they hated cusswords but thought women should shit or get off the pot. In a dream I was politely put on trial for failing to kiss one of them. No reply to an email, voicemail messages left and ignored, dropped into nothingness like coins down a deep well. I started dumping the emails in their own folder at some point and eventually noticed I had 108 of them.

I try to understand Oliver leaving—I understand anyone wanting to fall back to a better time, a more habitable world, and wanting to live quietly in the past. But he wouldn't have left simply for that reason, my Oliver. His cancer made the trip a requirement. Falling back is an effective cure. And what about memories, stored chemically in the brain? I like to think he will always remember our son Tomas, only a month old, his fingernails as small as pebbles, and his little fist, smaller than a plum gripping the end of my finger. Oliver had hovered over him, planting so many kisses on Tomas that he wondered aloud how many a baby could take. He wanted our son to live in love, shrugging off kisses like rain. How many kisses will ward off a stray bullet or thrown rock ten or twenty years later, waiting in time?

4: Athena

I MET OLIVER SO MANY YEARS AGO. AS RESEARCHERS early in our careers, we were sent to bright, flat Alaska to work quietly in a place thought to be out of the way. The grizzly bear under glass in the lobby of the hotel was always partly shrouded in glare, no matter how you looked at it. We rented a red Firebird and drove south to the Alaskan Wildlife Conservation Center where a Sitka black-tailed deer approached anyone and relentlessly licked them. Was it the salt? The bison and muskox sat around like people on couches in need of remotes, and a guest eagle sat perched on a tall branch, as calm as slow time. Nearby, a small fleet of halfway sunken houses was all that was left of Portage, a town destroyed in a 1964 earthquake. Peeling paint and doorways you must crouch down to look through. Surely someone grew up there, and maybe even lived an entire life there. We drove south to the town of Seward where the whole downtown is a few blocks of restaurants and souvenir shops, and stopped in a restaurant where a woman asked, "What are you doing here?" It wasn't exactly tourist season.

On the way back north to Anchorage we pulled into Beluga Point, and in the parking lot nearly stepped on a shotgun shell. Ah, America. What was there to do at Beluga Point but sit on the tallest rock like Buddha and have both our photos taken? The water alongside the highway had receded by that time of the day and left ice chunks the size of refrigerators.

Our next day off we took winding roads north to meet a man named Vern and go dogsledding. There were several more moose loitering in the snowbanks outside the entrance to his home and dog kennel. Oliver said they seemed as common as raccoons in Toronto. Vern was short, scruffy and bearded like a Civil War veteran from history books. We got out of the car surrounded by his barking dogs as he greeted us warmly, sized us up and decided we were fit enough to take turns standing as riders on the back of the dogsled. Normally he sat people in the sled and left it at that.

"It's a very peaceful way to travel," he said, and he was right. The dogs worked frantically but quietly, and we found ourselves gliding across the earth, though on a few occasions the sled didn't take the corners as easily as the dogs and we were pitched into a snowbank. As we got out of the snowsuits and various layers he'd given us, Vern asked if Oliver was an athlete, and I almost laughed—he was a researcher, after all—but he had apparently managed to cling to the back of the sled through turns that would have thrown a lot of people off.

Shaking hands with Vern, we drove further north to

see Denali, or Mount McKinley to the locals. We parked in Talkeetna and walked the one street it had, which is the closest I've ever come to feeling I was in the Old West. In the middle of town an old man was setting up a wheelbarrow so he could sit in it in the back of a pickup. Oliver warned, "I'm going to greet this man."

"Good afternoon, sir," was all he'd needed to say to open the floodgates: "Do you ever observe Mother Nature?" It was, we were told, important to look around, and we heard readings from his encyclopedia about the colour of sulphur at room temperature and the experiments "those old boys" did. He told us he often sat to observe jet trails, only once mentioning he was a Vietnam vet and leaving it behind in the torrent of information that lasted about ten minutes. We thanked him and made a polite farewell. Driving back to Anchorage, we went the wrong way on one-way streets and passed road signs marked by gunfire.

That was it, really, a brief friendship, but a friend you don't forget. We fell in step beside each other like two people who were meant to walk together all along. And a friendship that could have been more—he was curiously handsome, with a strong nose and a short, solid frame—but he was so deeply in love with Penelope. After that, I was granted a privileged position at Olympus Labs in Anchorage and he went back to Toronto. I had no time for romance or family, and felt like I was among the lonely gods, the exclusive manipulators. The money came pouring in but so did the scrutiny—staff were watched both at work and in our personal lives. I saw three moose in Anchorage loitering at the side of the road and chewing on vegetation and I joked in an email to Oliver that they were part of the surveillance.

Over the years, we dropped out of touch, and when I finally heard Oliver had been lost to us, I knew I needed to help the outside world learn more about what was happening and how things sometimes went wrong. I set up a meeting between his son Tomas—now twenty already—and a man I knew named Matthew. At the very least, it would be a start. I couldn't be too direct and risk exposure.

I appeared as Tomas to book a flight—it was a simple matter to step into the data-stream and create a hologram, borrowing photons and light and images of Tomas. Time would bend around me and resume its shape like a river around a rock. For the second that a clerk looked at my identification, the atoms in the flat plastic were made to look like his identification. I relaxed the effort and appeared as myself to mail the ticket and information to him, stepping out of a post office a few blocks from the family home in time to see Tomas for the first time. He rounded a sidewalk corner on his own to stop and look away from me down the street for a long minute. And then whatever it was, he simply let it drop from his mind. He was just like his father: strong, a dreamer.

5: Tomas

CHILDHOOD IS THE POOL THAT HOLDS ALL YOUR SE-crets, and yet you can't see to the bottom. I never adopted religion, but I found reverence among candles and a choir on Christmas Eve. The hard line of religion was different. It appeared in the form of a truck parked on my street handing out comic books about Christ with a huge splash of blood from the hand as he is crucified. I was too shy to approach the truck, but another kid went out to ask, "Can I have one for my friend?" and an arm reached out to provide it.

My mother regularly took me places and in subtle ways taught me reverence without getting too specific about the lesson. It didn't matter if it was Algonquin Park—we went there every summer—or the choir on Christmas Eve, I always assumed the idea was to know there are things great-er than yourself, and that in some way I should be there for the world, not just that the world is there for me. As a city boy, it had always meant a completely different ex-perience to drive north into the country, catching sight of a pickup with a bumper sticker that read TRUTH NOT

TOLERANCE. And you just know he's got a monopoly on the truth, that guy. The bumper stickers for sale at the general store in Kaladar, Ontario read, MISSING YOUR CAT? LOOK UNDER MY TIRES. I still remember the sign posted on personal property: THIS IS OUR LAND, BACK OFF GOVERNMENT. You don't even need to talk to someone to know you're somewhere different.

It was a curious thing to get a ticket in the mail for a flight to North Bay, and directions to a retirement home apparently purchased under my name. I had to think about what to do, though on some level I knew curiosity would win out.

Seeing the ticket brought back memories of going up north as a child, that peculiar open defiance of authority although people were frequently pleasant in person. As for myself, I had a certain amount of faith in authority, but only a certain amount. I didn't ultimately believe if a new and deadly virus came along I could just barricade myself in my house and discover a cure. We need government sometimes. At the same time, it took them months to determine that sending people back cured a terminal illness. And then the information wasn't immediately made public.

Suddenly, a terminal illness didn't take people away through death, but through passage into a new life. And then the rumours came that those wealthy enough could buy their ways back to live in peaceful times of their choice, and more environmentally stable times, quietly finishing their lives decades earlier, sometimes even in the same place they'd always lived. Never mind time-travelling assassins, the past was now a commodity. Maybe the end comes whenever you lose perspective, and the order of things. Most of us live in cities long enough to start thinking it's the beginning and end of everything, reaching around for something more meaningful only after the occasional disaster.

I had enjoyed camping in Algonquin as a child. There were always the unfortunate signs, the results of a path cut into the wilderness—a snake crushed on a dirt road, changing positions each time a car passed over it like a restless sleeper—but we did it to go home with a fragment of that peace in each of us, the sound of loons shivering across the water as a canoe dissects the lake. The sight of the rushes sticking out of the water near its edge like quivers of arrows, dragonflies the size of my thumb. The cliffs of the Barron Canyon Trail looking out on miles of pines determined enough to grow on hillsides and even down sharp cliff edges toward the water because life will be where it must.

6: Tomas

Nᴏʀᴛʜ Bᴀʏ ʜᴀᴅ ᴀ ᴍᴏᴜɴᴛᴇᴅ ᴊᴇᴛ ᴏɴ ᴅɪsᴘʟᴀʏ—ɪɴ-
teresting, but it would've been even more interesting if it
hung straight down like an animal in a butcher shop. It was
a curious and pleasant thing to see so much openness. I
was a creature of downtown Toronto, where the sky is ac-
companied by the hard, reflective mountain range of skyscrapers. Here I could see a Starbucks and other chain
stores scattered around like Christmas ornaments without a tree. It's good to remember many people live in more
open spaces, and can probably breathe more deeply.

Sometimes I'd just walk the streets in Toronto, or duck
into the subway to watch people. At rush hour they'd clus-
ter and scatter over and over again, odd patterns of people
that passed by unnoticed. Chewing gum makes anyone
look like an idiot cow. People would push and shove and
take my faith away, and then one kind gesture would re-
new it again. I rode subway trains torn between contempt
for people—all their fluttering, muttering and racing for
doors—and a strange admiration for this poorly trained

army, their defective but endlessly renewable charge, the wave of people that dig in every day but are sent home drowsy, clinging lightly to briefcases and bags, trying to manage a life in the off-hours.

I felt some envy for people who lived in a less constraining city like Montreal where the sky wasn't a set of ribbons, and where it seemed easier to pass a cathedral or somewhere else with some emotional space. Even getting outside the downtown core of Toronto helped, and I eventually settled near High Park.

My instructions directed me to Matthew and Helen in a North Bay residence for seniors. I couldn't remember them, but they were apparently old friends of my father. They were fixed in seats next to each other for hours at a time, both white and brittle things in a sparse cafeteria. They spoke slowly and pinched the air with small gestures. He said, "There were many problems with the experiments, with sending people back. Some people didn't arrive at the proper destinations."

His head nodded a moment before he continued. "Once travel started, it took a particular kind of concentration to fight the currents. People fell out of it, like someone falling off the back of a bumpy wagon. People were lost in time. Not all of them, but certainly some of them. I fell back a number of times and then stopped completely. Tried speaking to the media about it but they walked away thinking I was an eccentric old man. If someone were to return, I mean … find their way back still in the freshness of youth, people would have to listen, wouldn't they?"

I glimpsed a thin hand brush me and saw Helen wanted to speak. I leaned in to listen. With the larger ideas out of the way, she wanted to speak of more personal details. "Matthew had a brother," she said. "His name was Ackerley and he was among the lost, passing sideways through his own life." This made very little sense to me, so I asked her to explain. She sighed as though I were dense but smiled politely. "Matthew didn't get to his destination, where he was supposed to live with Ackerley, so we hired an investigator to look into it."

Another resident was stacking and fussing with plates not far away. I leaned in again to listen. "In the darkness and deep snow, he found himself outside a farmhouse owned by his wife's family. He'd spent many pleasant evenings there relaxing with her. He trudged happily through deep snow and pulled at the door but found it locked. Wanting out of the cold he went around the house knocking on windows, waving and moving on. By the time he'd come around to the door again, it opened and he was shot point-blank by another man—the man that had been her boyfriend twenty years earlier."

But most riveting to me was the scrap of information they had about my father. Matthew had heard that Oliver had lived somewhere in Scotland with a woman named Calandra.

7: Oliver

I'D NEVER BEEN TO MANHATTAN BACK WHEN I HAD my life, so it wasn't an unpleasant surprise to discover that's where I was the third time I fell back a few years. Slightly dazed, the first thing I did was step out of the pedestrian lane on the Brooklyn Bridge so that a cyclist had to brake. I said sorry but he just shook his head and rode on with me pegged. I went to the invisible scarf of smog on the observation deck of the Empire State Building, the fleets of hesitating cabs below no bigger than yellow candy bars on a rack.

New York is the Metropolitan Museum, the Museum of Modern Art, the Guggenheim, a saxophone player in Central Park and a fat man kissing ketchup off his hand in Battery Park with the statue in the distance. The square in front of Rockefeller Center looked like the ring on a rich man's hand, and so much of Times Square asked for your attention that none of it got any. The people were fascinating contradictions: parts of the city had the urgency of a cigarette on a bed, and yet three times as I stood looking at a map someone stopped to ask if I needed help. I watched a fit young businessman remove the top half of his suit and start a workout on a side street, and another man do contortions for spare change. A dumpy, middle-aged man glanced at me and narrowed his eyes. As he walked by, he held up a cigarette in one hand and a bottle of Coke in the other, moving his lips from one to the other, both held a few inches from his face.

There were people living out of shopping carts and rich old ladies with makeup caked on their faces as they walked tiny dogs. Whole groups of people at intersections were shuffled like a deck of cards and sent to another part of the city. On the subway people would make announcements that they were victims of domestic abuse and weren't proud to beg but needed to support a child, and they moved through the train with a hat. I watched a few guys quickly set up inside the doors and play drums between stops.

In the Cathedral Church of Saint John the Divine, you can find Poets Corner with an Elizabeth Bishop quote: *All the untidy activity continues, awful but cheerful.* I met Carl, a thin man who came in with a face the colour of ash and asked if I was a priest because I happened to be standing calmly with my hands behind my back. He'd lost his wife and daughter in an accident that spit them out of the car side by side on the road like a couple of factory items. He did most of the talking, but it was nice to be near another human soul and slowly, he began letting me say things.

Although he always spoke gruffly and was the sort of guy that said "spook" instead of "black man," I became his friend because I thought I could help him and because I didn't have any friends. He was the sort of man you could tell not to use a word like "spook" and he'd stop, rub his chin and say, "Yeah, yeah I guess." I trusted his loyalty, felt he'd never hurt anyone, and he was good enough to give me a couch in his simple apartment. He read voraciously but seemed to file the books away in his memory without impact, like photographs in an album he had no intention of reopening. I found several odd jobs and settled into an apartment of my own. One evening as we sat with coffee he suddenly asked, "What was the first book that really grabbed your nuts?" I thought about it and replied something about *Lord of the Flies* in high school.

8: Oliver

I'm losing Penelope. The memories of my old life are like a collection of islands, and every time I move on, it's as though the water level is higher. Maybe this was part of the design, to dull pain and allow for new lives in new locations. So, I'm writing things down: that we made love in a cemetery at night, the feel of the grass, and her body above me. In a discussion she said, "I think you're confusing your ideas," and folded her arms. I thought she was so smug I began childishly interrupting her. I want to keep her. I want the memories of her fanned before me so I can select from them.

Strolling around with Carl, we stopped at a sidewalk café and I suddenly noticed summer had given way to fall. I sometimes grew tired of Carl, but he was loyal like a dog. I began to see, depressingly, that it might take me years to get back home. Sitting outside in the summer I'd written feverishly in my notebook about Penelope, flipping to the back to make notes about my childhood, my foundation. My feeling was that if Penelope was drifting away, perhaps the rest of me would too and I'd lose my very identity. As a child I walked to school sometimes with a girl from my street named Emily and made her slow down or go ahead of me as we approached the school so that I wouldn't be seen arriving with a girl. Why did I do that?

I decided any friend of mine who came over to play should receive a bonus, and selected a handful of toys to give away when the time came. I thought it was an expert program to increase my popularity, but as I stood at the door saying goodbye to Emily, about to pass along a gift, my mother came swooping down to sharply explain, "Your friends are your friends because they like you." It was rare for her to lose her temper—most of my memories of her are of gentleness. When I was a toddler, she whittled my blue security blanket away by cutting off a strip at a time rather than taking it from me suddenly at once. It seemed like a good plan at the time, but she ultimately felt bad seeing me clinging to the only blue strip that remained.

I was the sensitive kid crying all the way to kindergarten on the first day, and nearly cried years later when she gently broke the news—as though there had been a death in the family—that Santa wasn't real, that he was only a symbol for goodness, the spirit of giving. Once, I sat in the back seat of a car about to go catch a film with some neighbours, and had to leave one of my mother's meals sitting unfinished. It suddenly struck me that she wouldn't always be there to cook these meals, and that I'd miss them someday. The whole concept of change and loss flooded me and I burst out crying, the father next door wondering what on earth was upsetting me. I wrote these memories down in the back of the journal and was tempted to tell them to Carl, but he tended only to listen carefully, nod and say little in return.

The next time everything began folding up and I felt myself beginning to fall again, I was on the sidewalk with Carl. Turning to him, I grabbed him by both arms and dug my fingers into his jacket. He looked confused but began to understand I was taking him with me and simply said, "Oh," as the drunk woozy feeling and shift in time hit him. Some part of me must have recognized I might need an army to get home and could build one from all the people lost to small corners of time.

9: Carl

Oliver talked too much, but I give credit where credit is due, and it's also fair to say he stood by his opinions and could explain them. Suddenly he grabs me like a lover and it's like falling off a cliff edge through life itself, trying for some measure of control by reaching for platforms of significant moments—the way you'd grab at outcrops on your way down a cliff.

And then I was standing on an incline listening to the gentle sounds of cowbells in the distance, mingled with the French language. We were in a town in the French Alps. We simply stood for a while inhaling the air. I would have to say it was refreshing to see humanity did not dominate the landscape, the small towns on other mountainsides spreading out like fireworks—a few short, clear lines in a handful of directions. With a little embarrassment we recognized we were pretty much in the side yard of a home owned by an elderly man. He emerged to stand in the doorway of his patio and look at us while his five dogs—all named after various nearby summits, we would later learn—pushed to get around him for a few seconds like something struggling to be born. As soon as they could, they shot in our direction, but he called them off.

He asked what we wanted and Oliver spoke enough French to converse with him. It turns out he was the local vet and worked in the town centre down a long, curving road. He seemed agreeable enough, and as I followed the conversation I kept looking up at the gathering clouds. I could tell it had stormed already once tonight and now the air felt loaded with the threat of more rain. Trees swayed, and as drops of rain began to arrive a tall man moved in a straight line down the road, and people moved with purpose like beads sorted on an abacus.

The man said his name was Julien and shook our hands. Perhaps in some way it helped that I kept looking at the sky because he ushered us inside to make tea and wait out the storm. He stayed in a manse attached to a church where the archbishop had lived, and he was alone. His wife was gone and his son had grown up and gone off to work as a doctor in Paris. He took us up the worn stone steps to a cluttered study that was glassed in on two sides, saying this was always the best way to view a storm. We watched it descend before it finally burst and thrashed at the windows while mist and cloud rolled in to cover every nearby mountaintop. It's a simple thing to say, but it may have been the most impressive storm I've ever seen. There are not many moments in life that make you feel like the hand of God is trying to find you.

The clutter of the office reminded me of a summer day not long after I'd graduated college and moved out on my own for the first time. My grandmother had died, and I was spending every Sunday helping my family clean out her home. A few weeks let loose a wave of garbage bags sent to the corner, furniture lifted to other homes and boxes of old photos lost in the shuffle. I'd overslept to discover my answering machine had recorded a call my brother made to see if I was coming. The recording went on minutes beyond his message to pick up the tick of an old clock, a crash and someone asking, "You okay?" I heard something like, "I can't even get the lid off," and my sister saying, "Carl might." My brother asked, "You don't want that trophy to keep? Winner!" and then, "Anything to do with food I think we should throw out, unless it's like … canned." Long minutes of hissing silence and rustling and then, "I'll put it by the card table," and "Garbage goes in bags not boxes, right?"

Julien let us stay, and it was a pleasant place. We made dinner together slowly every night as there was little else to demand our time. After a few glasses of wine one night, Julien commented that his son—the doctor—wanted to save the world but didn't send him a birthday card. And just as quickly he dismissed the thought with a wave of his hand in the air, changing the subject to his dogs. My favourite of his dogs was the brown one, a female, at first because I could tell it apart from all the black ones, but later for other reasons. Somehow it was the one that was both sad and pleasant; it was something in the eyes.

Of course, I thought of my wife and daughter, but we'd already fallen back the better part of a lifetime. And somehow to be displaced in time is to pull a curtain across your old life. They were so painful to think about; my mind had already started to reduce them to a series of prominent memories. If only I'd been hauled back a few years, or a few months, rather than a lifetime. Is it healing or a form of destruction to take the person you used to know and reduce them to that? I used to play with my daughter, both of us crawling around on the floor pretending to be cats. Who'd see the muted look of shock on my face now and picture me doing that? I thought of telling Oliver I wore a look of sadness for two people who'd not been born yet, but didn't want to offend him. He'd offered me friendship, and now he offered me a new life.

We stayed a year, but after that we began to grow restless. We grew tired of cooking in Julien's small kitchen where the flies from the neighbouring cows landed on everything. And as Julien drove us to town, all the sudden and winding turns made my stomach weak as though we were on a roller coaster. I knew what Oliver was thinking, and he knew that I was determining another member for our lonely team. We talked to Julien about coming with us when we fell, and explained it in a way that made us seem as sane as possible. I'm not sure he believed any of it, but he propped open the door a little and told us that if this thing was really happening, the dogs would get out and the neighbour would see to them. Finally, Oliver sensed it coming and I braced myself for it to happen again. I tried to help us stop more quickly this time. I dug my fingers into the soft bed of the past.

10: Penelope

I'VE ALWAYS HAD GOOD INSTINCTS FOR PEOPLE.
More than instincts: mild premonitions. When I was
a child, my father got cancer. He was a mild-mannered
lawyer, always in a black suit and a colourful tie, his one
method of expression. His hair had been grey forever but
otherwise he didn't look old. My mother began the process of worrying herself away, embracing an anxious state
of mind that concerned my father more than anything
else. It was as though she'd been replaced by a twitchy ac-
tress with the same soft, rolling brown hair. I simply closed
my eyes to think about it and knew he'd be fine. I pictured
him celebrating a birthday with me, years later, and after a
struggle that lasted about a year, he won.

But Oliver confused me. I hoped I'd know what to
think, but I saw him coming back and saw him settling
somewhere else. I spent four seasons alone, as any woman
newly separated should. A year alone is a way to get back
to yourself. In a way I think I was meditating on the loss,
aside from being busy with Tomas. Oliver left in the fall,

always my favourite season for the gentle reminder that change is a constant, and that everything is on the verge of transformation. After that, winter comes with its bright beauty and emphasis on hibernation and reconsideration. Spring is my second favourite season for the other side of the transformation, and summer makes me think of heat and frantic action. My preference is balance, either in spring or in the fall.

It was fall again, a year since Oliver left, when I tried Internet dating, only to abandon it after a few months. In the spring I met Blake at an audition for a commercial, both of us waiting for hours in a hallway with various others to prove we could smirk at a joke as we loaded laundry. He was a bit pale and his facial features looked somehow uneven, a little like they were drifting and trying to settle, but he dressed sharply and carried himself well. I was surprised and tempted to be offended when he asked for my phone number, but I provided it anyway.

Over a drink he said, "I noticed your gracefulness. I saw you in an audition before, but you didn't take the slightest notice of me while I admired the way you jogged up a few steps at a time, your arms showing a loose comfort with the rest of your body. It was the way your movements were smooth and your hair took the air. There are many attractive women, but the most astonishing ones also have other, unmistakable qualities, like comfort in their own skin."

Flattery is the most obvious, the oldest of techniques. It wasn't supposed to work, but I did feel like opening the possibility. He instinctively made me sense he'd be supportive and pleasant to be around, and in terms of the feeling it created, it was like using muscles I'd not used or thought about for a long time. I was cautiously intrigued. He said idiotically brilliant things like, "There's no one else like you."

He said anyone who could create a fable was tuned to the underground currents and deeper influences that help shape our lives. I told him, "If you'll excuse me, I need to go to the bathroom and make a current of my own." He laughed, but I could tell he was taken aback by the crudeness of my joke. I was, for the moment, tired of his pompous remarks, and felt like keeping him off balance. He handed me an envelope to read later and it turned out to contain a brief story he'd written about a young gypsy poet:

His mother named him Dukker, meaning fortune teller, and as a young man he said the strangest things about sunlight waiting patiently to get to the front of the line and touch his face, just for a second. He travelled, seeing London but not the rest of England, and was struck by a woman in red shoes stumbling down subway steps. He read great books and learned to cook a little. On trains he read about Nobel Prize winners even as boys behind him talked about wanting, wanting, wanting. From nowhere, a stranger turned to him and apologized, and within a year another simply commented that life could be worse than shaving, putting on a clean shirt and sitting around an apartment alone. He stood around train stations where sets of patient people crossed the floor and were swallowed by the city.

Walking with me to the station, Blake said, "You know, the city makes you choose. You glimpse a small man with wisps of straight black hair and watery eyes looking at nothing in particular, and you face a choice: love him or turn away. That's how the city kills warmth, one piece at a time." I had a fleeting thought about how the city has pockets of warmth, but people just didn't often feel so happy as to try and bond with a stranger. I felt like telling him he was full of it, but we'd reached a turnstile door made up of polished bars and I said, "Look, I've got to go," and he said he understood. He sent me a letter telling me he'd written an ending for the story about Dukker. The young man rejoins his family but one morning is simply gone. It's finally suggested a tree nearby hadn't been there before, that the young man had fallen and been transformed by earth, saying he'd let words wander away like so many coyotes. Let the world come to him.

11: Oliver

Julien needed a moment and was unsteady on his feet. We sat on a bench a while, and then blocks away met our preacher woman, Victoria, among the coloured houses and tilted streets of St. John's, Newfoundland. She had her hand on the stomach of a pregnant woman, a stranger she'd met while jogging, and was giving the child a blessing. "May your child that comes from love live in love, and know warmth and safety and joy." Victoria had short dark hair, a thin face and a wiry frame. She spoke calmly and remained perfectly still.

At first I had thought to scoff, but as we got a little closer I saw tears in the eyes of the pregnant woman. The woman hugged Victoria and walked away. We started to introduce ourselves, but Victoria said she needed to continue her run, so we jogged with her up to Signal Hill, which was far longer than any of us realized. Out of breath, leaning, we slowly took in the magnificent view and chatted further with Victoria. She revealed she had been a minister but had been forced out to live and work independently. I didn't want to demand more of the story, but took note to try to learn more when we'd earned more trust.

A week later, Victoria taught us greater subtlety. The next time we felt ourselves falling back, outside a pub on Water Street, she was a little out of reach and simply lifted an arm in our direction. Apparently, this intent was enough for her to fall back with us, and Victoria followed us gracefully to London a few years earlier. There were Carl and I clinging to Julien and each other like a couple of teenagers on a roller coaster ride.

We met the twin British boys—James and Aidan—when we found them standing on the steps to Westminster Bridge, not far from a statue of a lion that looked stunned. They asked, "Do you know where the closest groceries would be?" which Carl found hilarious, as much as Carl can find something hilarious. I admit that I cringed a little when Carl laughed. I'd never seen him laugh that hard. These two young men just stood there blinking like owls. They were both so thin they looked like they could slip under a wall.

One of them was born before midnight and the other after midnight, so they had different birthdays. They told us this with a slow and solemn manner, so everyone nodded. I looked at Carl so he would smother his laughter and nod too. Everything they said had a kind of honey-thickness, and I wondered if they'd be some kind of anchor the next time we fell back a few weeks later, but they weren't. Of course, we told them they'd fall back with us, and Carl and Julien in particular were good at looking serious and convincing about it.

Ferah was a young Turkish woman working in a dusty, small-town Spanish restaurant. On a patio made up of large, flat pieces of dry and cracked stone, we sat and ate before we eventually asked her to join us. She moved carefully but seemed curious. She was able to join us after the owner barked a few more orders in her direction over his shoulder. "I'm a student of history and philosophy," she said, pushing off from the table. We gathered her summer job here in this town had started to feel like a wrong turn and she'd prefer to leave.

Hearing the word *philosophy*, Carl couldn't resist the opportunity to tell her about the three-bullet theory. He'd told me this before and I resisted the urge to roll my eyes. "In a way, it's very simple," he said. "People would treat each other with better manners and civility if everyone carried a weapon and three bullets. The bullets would be engraved with a serial number that meant police could ask no questions if the bullet is found at the scene of a murder. As a result, everyone would be more polite. Seriously. You might not waste a bullet on someone rude in a grocery store, but few grocery clerks would want to take that chance. And some people who've lost all their bullets would need to bluff for the remainder of their lifetime, carrying around an empty gun. C'mon, you have to like the idea of a world with such civility." Carl wagged a finger at no one in particular.

"Civility," Ferah replied, "but only from fear, really, a kind of ongoing fear." Her green eyes moved back and forth from Carl to me, and while she had certainly put a pin in the balloon of his idea, the sharp point was softened by her genuine smile. "And black-market bullets could imitate the special ones and ruin everything," which left Carl stroking his chin and admitting the need to refine his theory. Ferah impressed me and spoke with us whenever she could for a few hours before finally walking off the job. The owner followed us a short way down the street ranting almost incoherently before the gravity of his business drew him back.

12: Oliver

We all stepped into the sunlight at a train station in Stuttgart, Germany to meet Maddy. She was a short, blonde woman in her thirties. She examined a sticker on a pillar and then made painstaking efforts to tear it off. She noticed us and said simply enough, "It's a sticker that argues multiculturalism means giving up power to others. You look lost and confused." She spoke flawless English and as she began to teach me a few phrases in German I started to feel she might join us as well. As we talked mostly in English, a pale older man worked his way over. "Excuse me," he said. "I know you speak English but here in Germany we speak German." He spoke as a train rolled into the station. He paused to look at us and then stepped onto the train to be carried away. Maddy fumed. "That's really rude," she said. I decided to be fair—it's possible to meet a creepy man in any country.

I sensed we'd be here longer. In the first few days, before we all began to settle into apartments in the same neighbourhood, we went to a lot of restaurants. Germany began to feel like a country of sharp contrasts: one waiter spoke coldly and his eyes were hidden behind glasses that sometimes caught a reflection as another smiled, barrel-chested, his woodpecker-rapid laugh ready on a hair-trigger.

A year unfolded. I liked Stuttgart for its open parks and public squares, a pedestrian street and a twittering tree filled with birds I couldn't see. A store announced the "Year of the Scots" sale, a cartoon man in a kilt slashing the price. The Scots were, it seemed, synonymous with cheapness. We visited a folk festival with beer tents, rides, huge mugs of beer and rumours of waitresses in Munich who could carry eight on a tray with one hand. Learning German was challenging and I began to appreciate the difficulties of someone new to a country, trying to build a life. It was a language with a sharp beauty, but it stuck in my mouth like twigs. Maddy had a boyfriend named Aldman—a name that means *old man*—and he was as patient as Maddy when it came to repeating German words until they began to take up residence in my brain. Aldman worked in a bookstore, and while bookstores still drew me in like a magnet, I found that in foreign countries I could only stare at the covers and guess at the contents.

As Aldman took a break from work, a few of us stood around eating pretzels off a pretzel stand. Maddy fixed me with a stare and told me a British tourist had yelled something at her along the lines of, "Your breasts proceed you like a motorcycle escort." I looked at Ferah, speechless for a couple of seconds. Part of it was the absurd politeness of "breasts," even as he was appallingly inappropriate. Aldman only laughed and rolled his eyes. He was one of those huge, gentle people. In some ways the world is the same everywhere.

We visited Schorndorf, *Tübingen* and Cologne, which had a magnificent cathedral, its walkway buffeted by wind and every inch covered in graffiti. Black-and-white postcards in racks on the street showed the city after the war, devastated except for the cathedral. Maddy's kindness contrasted with a glimpse of a pack of skinheads on the street, walking through the fog with their tall leather boots and assorted dogs. We heard about a Molotov cocktail thrown into a synagogue, impressive arts festivals, and I will never forget sitting with Maddy and Ferah on a bench somewhere along Philosophers' Walk above Heidelberg as all the bells of the city rang at once.

I was on a train to the wine region town of Neustadt with Carl when we stopped and I looked out the window to see a lanky skinhead on a bench, his girlfriend draped over him. He looked up and smiled a sick grin, and I turned back to my book, unable to engage him. Long minutes later we were finally on our way again and a conversation began in our compartment, an old man telling stories about tollbooth castles along the Rhine and opposite castles run by two brothers who hated each other. He talked about a woman who distracted sailors by combing her long golden hair. He spoke to a friend who translated for him and turned his head away shyly each time I looked over. I went through my phrase book and as I stood to leave, managed to say quite perfectly, "It was nice meeting you." He beamed at me and asked where I was from. When I said Canada, he listed on trembling fingers the parts of Canada he'd seen.

I began to sense we'd be falling again soon. It was time to get everyone together. But I was glad I'd been there. Canadians aren't taught anything about Germany at school. We're given a steady diet of information about the world at war, a tiny river of black-and-white carnage in the mind. History can't be forgotten, but I felt glad to have new realities: a gentle smile from Aldman, filed away under Germany.

13: Athena

IN THE END, THERE WERE AROUND A DOZEN OF THEM.
I couldn't always see what Oliver was doing as he gathered
his small army. The data pooled and collected. I caught
up with them, or could at least monitor them most of the
time, though sometimes they moved behind dense thickets of activity and living history like fish moving out of
sight in an aquarium. Put all kinds of whispering days in
one room, and the noise is deafening.

As head of the program, Dr. Waters has a tendency
to come sweeping into any room as though he owns the
place, his white hair and beard making him look like a
madly alert grandfather to us all. I've only seen him outside the facility once, standing on the street and wearing
a hornet-yellow helmet while holding a bicycle, a small,
red brick house behind him with checkered curtains in
the windows and a cloud that appeared to be coming out
of the roof. I thought maybe it was where he lived, but he
simply stared down the street, mounted his bike and rode
away without seeing me.

Waters said he could see data patterns, tunnels of lived experience. As soon as one person finished watching an old film noir, another person began it, leaving patchwork lines like trenches across time where men hesitate in shadowed doorways forever, or are slapped across the face again and again. Waters winced and turned away at centuries of wife beating, and laughed for long minutes at the sound of happy babies. Some said his discoveries had driven him mad, but I didn't agree. He was doubtless eccentric and seemed foolish at times, but it was a mistake to underestimate how sharp-witted he could be, or how physically spry. He sometimes spoke in poetic fortune cookies, his own curious shorthand. He said, "A lifetime is something that sails in and out of the crowded room of the world as briefly as a gurney on little squeaking wheels that hope to be remembered."

With him staring at my computer screen, suspended over my keyboard and staring like a gargoyle, we worked together to gather more data about Oliver. In Mexico City they met a theatre-maker and clown named Fernando as he practised in a park. He wore minimal makeup but colourful shirts with black pants and tall boots, pulling his hair back into a ponytail to highlight his sharp features. They watched a black dog run across green grass, thinking it belonged to Fernando, but the dog simply kept going. Fernando was calm but curious, like a cat, and seemed to inspire as much in those around him.

They were together as a group when they walked into a soft trap, a place called Club Lotus, where the drinks were often spiked and people were robbed. They'd have been obvious targets, giving themselves away as new in town. They arrived in Verona and were close to the Lotus on their first night in the city, Oliver leading his dozen people like a disorganized scouting party through the streets. Dr. Waters had left me alone and so I intervened, appearing in the form of a short, middle-aged restaurant owner in a dark blue suit with a round face. As they arrived on foot I caught their attention and pointed out the owner's place down an old alley. It had a small patio that always had fresh flowers. In gregarious fashion, I told Oliver, "You look like a man who appreciates a good restaurant!" I shook Oliver's hand and walked away. I knew Oliver, and knew to be pleasant not pushy, though I think he suspected something and caught a hint of my real mood as I tried to walk away thoughtfully, my round face an awkward mask in the moonlight.

14: Victoria

We found ourselves in Germany again, and Oliver thought if a pattern was developing it was best we try and make it something of our own making. We'd leave Germany and take a train to Italy. I thought of myself as the conscience of the group, but saw no reason to object to this, even if I couldn't quite follow the logic. The train jerked to life with all of us aboard and creaked toward Italy. A Middle Eastern man who'd been helpful with our bags issued a small prayer as the train began to move. I smiled and nodded at him and he smiled and nodded back. I felt sure he'd say another prayer of thanks when we arrived, and thought there was something remarkable about unabashedly producing evidence of one's gratefulness.

I sat across from Julien, Ferah and Fernando and tried to tell them my feelings about trains and platforms as the train arrived at each new station: "Some elements are universal to every station. People waiting on platforms flash like photos as we arrive, our window sailing boldly in and collecting them like a child scooping up toys. Look, a woman holds back a newspaper and slides away into a man pressing on the earth with a cane, though most simply stand and stare. Notice the eyes. A little wider than usual, they come forward first, beating around for a path, stretching back to the uncertain."

Looking at Julien, I saw that he seemed hesitant, but Ferah and Fernando were interested. "Look," I said. "The train begins to slow and they all step forward expecting the future, or as if someone were going to give a speech." "What are they asking for?" Julien wanted to know. I could only answer, "They all have their own needs. Look at me. I needed a new family and met all of you."

Colourful Verona had a Dante statue in one piazza, and the Juliet balcony had nearby walls covered in hopeful and desperate graffiti, tourists everywhere. At the amphitheatre, a middle-aged tourist with an umbrella sang spontaneously, walked away to a smattering of applause, paused, and then walked back and sang again. He repeated this a few times, apparently deciding each time it was a lovely little moment, and that he should go and have it again. The Verona station had more multiculturalism than we'd seen in some parts of Germany—Maddy reminded me that racism was better able to thrive wherever there was a monoculture. We saw three gypsy children—the girl looked very tough—and we climbed the twelfth-century Torre dei Lamberti for a view of the city. A man with a round face and blue suit spoke to Oliver and recommended a local restaurant where I ate a dinner of penne with four cheeses, and pizza with ham, sausage, artichokes and mushrooms. I drank Limon chino, which was like a small glass of sunlight.

We piled into cabs to get to the hostel Oliver had arranged for us, and as we slowly passed it in a small burst of traffic, my eyes caught on a slim, neon sign for a bar called Club Lotus, hanging in a set of long dark windows framed by heavy stones. For a few seconds it felt as though we'd been to this city together before, had visited this place or had even been there tonight. I knew this was absurd, but a feeling is a feeling. I've never felt comfortable in bars and always thought it funny the word had another meaning: *steel poles meant to restrain.* Clubs has pretty much the same double meaning. I guess you could say I only sometimes fit into bars.

But I had a momentary vision of all of us in this place, music heavy in the air. Through the windows I could see the haze and squirm on the dance floor where a tall man danced an awkward crane dance, dressed all in black. He found what looks good on him. Other men stood in one place bobbing up and down with their knees and looking around like lost sailors. It looked like there was a fireplace, plush chairs and video screens. I saw Carl with his thin frame swallowed by a chair so that I could see only part of his head, his hands and his feet. He looked like he wouldn't be able to move again. The British twins and the German couple stood around at the bar talking and laughing.

And just for a second, I saw a woman that could have been Sara. She was sitting at a table, smiling at what must have been a joke, her wrist going limp and cigarette short enough to be a glowing ring. Her foot lifted sharply under the table like an animal lifting its head at a noise. It seemed the only part of her that wasn't self-conscious. If only that joke had been so funny that instead of a measured smile she dropped laughter, letting it shatter like a plate. I wanted a thread that I could pull to unravel her and see the real person. If it was the real Sara, it was the only thing that could keep me in this city. I left the church for her when crucial people objected to the relationship. I didn't lose my faith, but I lost my faith in the church. And then it simply didn't work out—and I don't believe in allowing regret into your home—but for a long moment I saw her again.

We were all in there and then we weren't. It happened and it didn't happen. We went there, but we didn't because we listened to the man with the round face. All of this flashed through my mind in the moment that I craned my neck and watched the thin, neon sign sail by and slip out of sight.

15: Oliver

From Verona we took the train to La Spezia. All of us were talking excitedly except the twins, James and Aidan, who had the odd habit of napping at the same time, leaning together like a couple of tent poles while Aldman looked them up and down curiously. I eventually assumed they didn't want to miss each other, even when they slept. As a group, we wondered if the change in geography meant being off our prescribed path, and somehow more able to take control. I knew Penelope and Tomas waited for me across a period of time as wide as any bright ocean, and that if I returned home with these good people it would be clear how many were lost, how much had gone wrong.

The Gulf of Poets was known for attracting Byron, Lawrence, Shelley and others, but as we walked down the main street at 1:30 in the afternoon, it was completely dead. We all wandered near the waterfront when an old man in a suit paused in front of me as I sat on a bench, and tried to guess where I'm from. "England? America? Russia?" I said, "No… No…" When I told him I was from Canada he said,

"Oh, Canada is magnificent. Italy has absorbed everything bad, has been a test since 1945." I thought to ask what he meant by that, but he was already making other rambling statements. He paused only to spit away a piece of chocolate clinging desperately to his lip. "Keep your bright eyes," he said. Then he went twenty feet away, came back, and said, "The most important things are the heart and the brain—follow the heart but when you need the brain, use it."

We left for the five villages—climbed the tower in Vernazza to watch the crashing waves, and walked the hill toward Monterosso where a skinny black cat tried to kill a pigeon as a tourist photographed the small, frantic battle. At night from a small stone and metal balcony, we watched the moon fight free from the clouds and illuminate parts of the water. A few skinny cats between villages ate all our cheese and one of them scratched me to give thanks. Each beautiful town had similar geography, but a different setup of docks and boats. I thought these towns introduced a new way of thinking: all the colourfully painted houses built into the hills in steps so that the next street was up or down from wherever you stood.

When we returned to Vernazza the old man was, to my surprise, looking for us. I stopped thirty feet from him on the street and watched as he locked eyes on me and raised his arms as though trying to embrace me. He said, "I have been forward and I have been back, and now I choose to be back." Together, the two of us returned to the tower and as we walked he said his name was Antonio. I asked him if he meant that he had drifted as we were drifting. He said he knew we were falling back; he could see it in our expressions as someone who had done it himself. "It was over a freshly killed light," Antonio said, "that the shadows leaped together and tied up into darkness, and it was always in bed I was pulled back. My mind was like a child on the beach, turning over rocks and pushing through sand for hard shells, unable to dwell on the past and looking for memories. I felt it brush around me and waited for the pull of movement into the past, but I found a way around this."

He had created a placebo effect with a simple leather bag he considered the focal point of all his thinking on the future. He had assorted meaningful things in the bag: his wedding photo, a watch that belonged to his grandfather and a book from his childhood. "It is enough to tell me I already stand on the past," he said. Concentrating on this, he was able to slow his progress into the past and even move forward a little. "We need not be dragged down by the stones in our memory," he continued, "if we already hold them before us." I understood instinctively that my friends needed to think much more on this idea for it to work. Maybe Antonio had tricked his own mind but I couldn't count on all of us managing it. Antonio raised his hand, insisting he had settled and wouldn't come with us. He said he had mastered the winds and didn't need to carry on. With few other options, I returned to my friends explaining that Antonio was a brilliant engineer and the bag contained a device that would help us return.

A month later, my mistake was in giving it to the twins to carry as we once again began to feel the current of movement come around us, knowing it meant another fall. I felt all of us lift and begin to fall back with the familiar scream of history around us. And then miracle of all strange miracles, we stopped and held our ground. I almost laughed out loud with joy but was afraid of breaking the spell. Again, I almost laughed when I thought of Antonio saying, "Your mind can be a clear lake, but someone will still want to piss in it." And then it all fell apart. In the corner of my eye I saw the twins open the bag, one of them running a hand around inside it and appearing confused before we were all thrown back to our starting point in Vernazza as though we'd never left. We hit the ground hard and there were scrapes and bruises. The twins were gone. We'd separated from them as they clung to the bag. Carl scoffed at the idea it could have worked, and from the expressions on the faces of Julien or Maddy, they agreed. Our chance had slipped away; we would miss our two watchful owls.

16: Oliver

IN FLORENCE THEY CUT THE PIZZA SLICES AS BIG AS you want them, and there were tiny lizards at home on warm stones. We spotted the Duomo but got lost dodging traffic in an attempt to work our way over to it. In the first few days, our visit to Florence was a blur of culture. I stared and stared at the veined, stone hands of statues. These were some of the most animated statues I'd ever seen, but the effect could be temporarily ruined by a bird jumping from an astonished face to an outstretched finger. Standing before *The Rape of the Sabine Women* by Giambologna, a tourist from somewhere in North America stopped, put his hands on his hips and pronounced, "Looks like some hanky-panky going on there." Even the war memorial was animated, not simply a standing soldier but a man holding the slumped body of a friend who pointed his rifle.

We broke up into groups to see the city. I liked the piazzas, the old covered bridge, the Palazzo Vecchio, the River Arno at night catching the reflection of lanterns and the moon, even as the buzz of every Vespa on the road intruded on the scene. The next morning we saw the Basilica di Santa Croce and the tombs of Michelangelo, Galileo and Rossini. The tourists moved in masses like whales around the Bargello and Basilica di San Lorenzo, and I loved that people of all ages mixed, sitting on the many steps of the Piazza della Santissima Annunziata. In the Galleria dell'Accademia—an hour's wait to get in—I turned a corner and saw *David*. It looked to me like perfection and I felt emptied and filled with a cool, clear liquid.

"I'm a culture monk," Fernando said, "and this is a little like being given water when you didn't know you were thirsty." It was a cool, perfect evening and we all met again at a square on the west side of the city. I had no idea we were about to meet a man unlike any other man who took air out of the world. Looking across the street I saw a yellow building, only several storeys, with bushes along the front lawn surrounding the wide-open double doors. Inside the doors was a deep darkness like a cave. I could see no sign, but thought it must be a hotel, and felt magnetically drawn to it. I led all my precious friends up the steps and through the doors.

We found an open, comfortable lobby area with couches and chairs. A wide counter ran down the middle of the room and displayed flowers, bread, cheese and fruit. There was only one other exit at the back of the room: a door coloured a simple grey, like ash. It did not appear to have a handle, so I assumed it might slide open. There were a few windows along the wall, but heavy drapes covered them.

I felt the same curious light humming in the air I'd not known since I stood before the original door that sent me back, away from my Penelope. There was a sense of reversal, a sense that the forces that caused erosion—either in the land or the body—were forced to hide like criminals. We were spread out throughout the room when Carl turned toward me to say, "We should leave. This doesn't feel right."

But I disagreed, saying we should have a look around. I thought there was something useful to be found here. He gave me a brief look I couldn't easily define and turned to look around the room with the rest of us. I joined Maddy, who had found a computer terminal with an inviting message indicating the place was expressly designed for travellers. The message assured us someone would be here shortly and invited us to enter our names and places of origin. Maddy entered, "Nobody."

A minute later something slid closed to block the double doors at the entrance. I glanced around at the looks of concern from my friends and approached the shadowed entrance to find a wide, seamless grey door. In the darkness of the entranceway, one small, red spark stood out from somewhere near the ceiling. I stepped closer and saw that it was a camera's eye protected by a transparent dome. It sat clinging to the ceiling where it could easily survey the room. The dim light inside the dome was strong enough to reveal two thick, black wires resting on either side of the mounted camera like grotesque hairs. Taking another step toward it, I nearly jumped when a severe voice emerged from speakers perched somewhere in the same dark entranceway: "Touching an electrified door isn't a very pleasant thing—it would be advisable to stay back." There was a pause as my friends and I looked around at each other, all of us startled. The voice continued, "What sort of travellers are you that don't eat food and explore a room?"

I briefly considered saying we were looking for a way home, but it would have been far too complicated. Instead I said, "We're good-natured travellers looking for rest, and we might find we have much to discuss. At the very least, we expect to be treated as you would hope to be treated yourself." There was only a short pause before he replied, "My instruments see raw time on you, and perhaps you can smell it in the air here yourself. It becomes something you carry with you. And you lie by leaving out so much of the truth of your situation. I know who you are. You are some of the pebbles time kicks beneath its feet. Nobody will even miss your absence."

"Wait," I said, but the moment he finished speaking, the smaller grey door at the back of the room slid open, and with the first tug of air whistling out of the room in the direction of the open door, I felt a horrified pang at what was happening. We all turned to look. Carl was closest to the door. It had opened behind him and he raised his arms in an attempt to keep his balance in the fierce wind that pulled him through. Beyond him and through the door we could see the same soft, translucent shapes we had seen the first time we stepped back through time.

Carl jerked and bent forward, and then was at the door, his hands clinging to both sides of the frame. I glanced around and saw all the others grabbing the counter or chairs to stay where they were. For a few seconds I thought Carl would simply be sent somewhere else and there might be hope of retrieving him, but the system here had been modified. He began to scream and his body hideously stretched out as it was pulled in hundreds of tiny rivers of possibility. My instincts and experience told me enough: he had been dissected by time.

The door slid shut and we released our grips on whatever had held us fast. Maddy and Julien dropped to their knees; the rest stood in stunned silence. I made my way over to a nearby chair and sat down. Carl had been my closest friend in this strange, new life and I was numb. Everyone gathered near me, at least partly because I had been on the other side of the room, farthest from the smaller door. It was a long moment before I raised my head, but as we were all tired, I said only, "We need a plan. And we should sleep on this side of the room, as far from that door as possible."

That night we lay together on the safe side of the room like planks in a raft, each within arm's reach of another, the occasional soft murmur of a conversation like the gentle lap of the sea around us. Carl was just the person I wanted to advise me at this moment and I felt I'd disappointed him. We could see the dull, red eye of the camera in the darkness and spoke quietly in the hope that the source of the voice could not see us or hear us.

For long hours we speculated about why this had happened. I finally hypothesized out loud, "We know someone has attained the carefully guarded secret of time travel. That person must be experimenting with this secret, and experimenting on people like us while being safely hidden in the past where nobody has any idea that these things can be done." In agreement, Fernando said in his hesitant English, "I think the moment Carl was taken, the moment he went in a lot of directions, I think it must provide a wealth of information."

"Either for scientific use or because some bastard enjoys it," Victoria added. "Or both," Aldman said. "I think the incredible winds are because a safety feature has been removed," was all I could think to add, but suddenly I was frustrated with our useless speculation and felt a hard kernel of anger within me. Rising to my knees, I felt Fernando and Aldman reach out to grab my arm and belt, but I was too busy pulling together my thoughts and directing my voice at the hateful red eye. "Who are you? By what right do you do this, coward? And for what purpose?"

There was a long pause and I began to assume I'd get no answer when a voice said, "As you'll all find your way through the far door sooner or later, it doesn't matter if I tell you. Paul is my name and I'm working to give people what they want: enough data to know exactly how to change the past. Your friend had a curious personality." I don't remember what I said next but I certainly stammered and screamed and told him he wouldn't know how to live a good life if his life depended on it, before the urgent, pleading hands of my friends successfully brought me back to the ground to quietly talk of escape.

In the morning we moved slowly, crawling to try to reach the food and find anything in the room we could use to our advantage. The furniture was bolted down, which was why none of it had moved when Carl was taken from us. Closer to the door, Maddy and I discovered a heavy, plush chair that was loose with a couple of the legs partially unbolted. I tried not to think about how many people had tried to hang on to it before they were pulled to their deaths. "A pocketknife?" Maddy requested. Fernando crawled over with a knife that belonged to Aldman. I left Maddy and Fernando to work on prying loose the remaining legs so we could use the chair to try to smash a window on the far side of the room by the double doors and the endlessly watching, tedious eye.

I was moving to check on Ferah when Julien half-stood and knocked a platter of food to the ground. The door pulled open again. Julien resisted, but our patient enemy had excellent timing and Julien was jerked back in the direction of the door. From my position on the floor I watched, horrified as Victoria stood and reached out to him in a snap decision that cost her everything. He reached out to her too, but only pulled her off her feet and the door took them both.

For a long time we lay still, and then I began to move back toward Fernando. "Keep going," I said. "Lift your head and continue to work on getting the chair loose." Hours passed, but when the chair was loose we did our best to drag it along the floor without standing. Fernando raised himself up a little and the door opened so that again the furious wind arrived. Acting on an impulse, I turned my body and kicked the chair so that it bounced once, and went through the open door.

The wind stopped instantly and white flashes of light pulsed a strange rhythm. Whatever shifting, translucent images we could see through the door drifted into nothingness. The doorway settled back into a simple door but remained open. I thought I heard a dull explosion from behind the wall. A light twist of smoke made its way into our room. A man emerged, whom I could only guess to be Paul. He was a tall, pale creature with wisps of black hair clinging to the side of his head. Using one arm to cover his face and eyes, he cried, "I'm blind!" In a string of curses and half-finished sentences, he made it clear our chair had destroyed a system designed only for organic life.

A sleepy, computerized voice was trying to sound the alarm. Using the name Maddy had entered, it kept saying, "Warning: Nobody has caused an overload and uncontained fires." By now we were all standing, and to our astonishment, saw that the main entranceway behind us was open. Paul must have thought to try and make his way out to seek medical help but only worked his way over to a wall, helplessly feeling around as we backed through the now open door. Fernando made a move toward him, but I held his arm and announced to Paul, "You deserve nothing less for all you've done. Tell any poor fool who will listen that Oliver took his payment for the loss of his friends."

I wanted him to know my name while he lived and suffered, though even as we made our way out to spill into the street, I regretted having given it to him.

17: Athena

Dr. Waters could never hide his emotions. When he returned to work after his son was blinded, his body wore his anger like a flag. I heard his angry cries, muted only slightly by my office window, and eventually learned the details. Waters wasn't terribly clear at first, only saying that his son had been injured somewhere in the past, where he had been engaged in his own research. It must be a strange thing to have your son injured before he was even born, a time that had previously been only a quiet stretch of history for you. It was one of the curious impossibilities brought to our lives by the discovery of time travel, that a father can find out his son was injured or killed in the past, and didn't just worry for the future. It became another wrong-headed undercurrent in our lives, as quiet and disturbing as the buzzing of a hornet in the next room. Lives that could be eliminated in a nuclear flash, lives not based on clean energy. Each challenge never anticipated, more pervasive, more complicated.

I eventually learned from someone else on the project that Waters was after a traveller named Oliver—otherwise my reaction might have betrayed to Waters that I knew him. Waters reassigned people to track down Oliver and his friends with little care that they had suffered losses of their own. But I found them first. Feeling they should move again, and to try and take their minds off their losses, they went to Siena and the Piccolomini Library to see the frescoes. They spoke little and sat eating in the square, forming up into a neat pile of umbrellas, the only ones under a drizzle of rain and a muted sun veiled by mist and cloud. Next, they decided to take the train to Rome and as the trees and countryside passed, Maddy joked, "Our travel days are always brilliant. It's as though a visit to a train station stops the rain." It was an attempt to lighten the mood but it had failed. I saw the expression Oliver wore as he looked at Maddy leaning into Aldman. I know he was trying not to feel jealous of the comfort they could give to each other.

In Rome, men dressed as gladiators stood outside the Colosseum and posed with tourists. Oliver seemed impressed with the broken remnants of history everywhere— ruins and semi-pillars. They split up to explore different parts of the city. Oliver was sitting in the Pantheon with Fernando when a man of about sixty spoke to them in Italian. He had a pleasant, lined face and thinning grey hair. Oliver said, "Non parlo italiano," and the man smiled gently and spoke in slow English, "Welcome to my country in this place." He showed them around the city for hours.

They stood in front of fountains and Oliver learned he was a sculptor and that he had a daughter in Ireland married to a composer. They stopped for coffees. Oliver went out of his way to scramble for money and pay for them before the older man could. "I will remember this night!" said the man with a pleasant smile and walked away, nearly bumping into someone on the street. He simply smiled again, gave another little wave and went on. Oliver and Fernando strolled around, and Oliver said he felt lightened to have met a good soul.

As a group, they were now much more cautious. Maddy and Aldman had seen a poster for a resort and volunteered to visit it the following day in advance of everyone else, to be certain it was safe and to see if they might stay. It was an old, stone house surrounded by wide grounds. They passed a gate of polished stone. Carved into the stone, wolves and lions lay on either side of the path and caught small pockets of sunlight to spin gently around and release. Inside, impressive topiary met them as they followed the path to the house. A squirrel the size of a dog sat sculpted into one bush and a bird the same size sat on the opposite one. "I hope we aren't getting into something odd," Aldman said.

Catherine answered the door: a striking woman with long red hair that moved in waves and green eyes. She smiled as she greeted them, much warmer than any tired traveller could have expected from a stranger, saying, "Come inside and add your happiness to the world."

She led them to a comfortable dining table and her staff brought cheese and wine, and as they talked and ate,

Maddy and Aldman found their will melting away into a relaxed state like none they had ever known. Reality mixed with illusion, and Maddy imagined the polished stone wolves and lions coming to life to lie at her feet and nudge her hand. Drugged, they became extremely susceptible to suggestion, and when Catherine tapped them on the shoulder saying, "Now, go and fill yourself," they obeyed without hesitation. Leaving the room, they entered the grounds. They found scattered others feasting, drinking and following all other instincts.

During this time, Oliver remained with Ferah and Fernando. They sat for hours, becoming more and more tired until dusk and rush hour arrived. Finally, Oliver announced, "We need to follow them and try to discover their fate," but I couldn't let him approach that same house and fall into the same situation. I worked with several close and trusted colleagues to borrow images of a man throughout the years. Nobody famous. In life, a businessman and father of two. His name found its way into a newspaper once. We took him from among the millions of overlooked and used his image: a tall body, dark eyes and sharp features. He lived a long life, and there were many images of him lifting a child or squinting into the sun. His name was Herman. We gave him peace and our words. He was a man made by others from everything we knew of him, a temporary man as they all are.

We arranged for Herman to be on a particular street corner so he would meet Oliver. It was a busy corner but a hurried crowd so indifferent it may as well have been a private conversation. Herman stepped in his path, raised a hand to stop him and said, "Athena sent me."

"Athena? Really? How is my old friend?" Herman replied, "She is well, though she risks much in bringing you this, an antidote to the drug your friends have been given." He held up a small vial and offered it to Oliver, who took it before Herman added, "Catherine owns the place your friends have visited and will greet you warmly but serve drugged food that induces a desire to stay forever in comfort. If you take the antidote first, you'll be able to greet her and eat the food, but stay alert and catch her by surprise." Herman then stepped away with the rush-hour crowd. He fell into the corner of an eye, the back of a mind.

Oliver seemed a little taken aback, but after walking a few blocks he smiled a little and I could only assume he felt reassured by help from an old friend. I was relieved to see him open the vial and drink the contents as he passed the stone gate and the growing shadows of dusk. When Catherine answered the door, Oliver appeared struck by her beauty and warm smile, but he also appeared to check himself, pausing at the door to glance around and no doubt remind himself this woman held two of his friends. She led him to the same dining area as the others were led; wine and cheese were served and she asked him about himself. Oliver ate and offered little conversation, instead pushing for Catherine to speak. She said, "My land here is a resort, that's all. It's dedicated to comfort and the brand of enlightenment people find here."

When they had talked a while and Oliver had eaten and drank, she stood and went to him to tap him on the shoulder, saying, "Now go and fill yourself." But Oliver stood abruptly. Anger trickled into his eyes. "Who are you that you need to drug people and keep them against their will?"

"I keep nobody against their will," Catherine replied and agreed to take Oliver to his friends, explaining that the drugs only made people most agreeable and interested to consume. Oliver persisted, saying he had traces of the antidote left and would go to the police. Passing through the building he saw people eating, drinking and taking each other by the hand upstairs. He followed Catherine out into the open grounds where they found Maddy napping in a patio chair. Next, they went inside for Aldman. Catherine led them up plush, winding steps to a higher floor before she gestured vaguely at a door and said, "Aldman." It was a white wooden door and Oliver tapped softly a few times before he opened it. Inside, Aldman lay sprawled across a bed with a woman they didn't recognize. Maddy smiled.

As they descended the stairs Oliver asked Catherine what she meant by all this. She sighed as she gracefully descended the steps, explaining, "Some call this a cult, not a resort, but I prefer to think of it as a temporary station of sorts. Those who want to accomplish little never find the motivation to throw it off and leave, and the world is better without them. Your friends are not shallow and were already starting to show signs of resisting. They'd have left on their own free will soon."

Catherine suggested, "Stay, and find yourself stronger for having pulled free of this place when you want to go." She served food free of the drug. In the end, they stayed a month. Oliver called for the rest of the group to join them, trusting the stay would involve no more tricks and knowing the group needed a break. It was only Ferah who stood inside the door cautiously, and when Oliver assured her that all was well, replied, "You said that before and people died." Oliver took a step but restrained himself, particularly as Maddy and Aldman intervened. "Oliver has good instincts," Maddy said, "and shouldn't be faulted for the surprise that overtook us before."

It was a peaceful and restful time for them. Fernando and Maddy made a short play based on her experience working in a bookstore. It was a comfortable store with wide windows that let in the sunlight and Fernando held hoops that he moved gracefully through the air to represent the movements of the planets. Maddy told about books sometimes falling off the shelf, fluttering to the ground like tired bats. "The books are leaping off the shelf today," she'd say. The seasons came and went, people who called themselves important struggled for power, but the books remained the same. "There is Dickens, the words curled up like sleeping rope." Fernando emerged wrapped in newspaper and slowly burst out as Maddy read assorted statements that sounded like headlines but were not.

The time finally came that Oliver felt they'd be falling back again soon. A day later he felt the gathering tides and the slow, oncoming approach of a fall when they lost Fernando. He'd had enough and walked away. They watched him turn and wave, wearing one of his typically colourful shirts and smiling his genuinely warm smile before the curious, displaced feeling met their senses and they slipped away. When they fell back again, Waters found them. I'll never forget looking over my shoulder to see his expression, very much the way a cat would look before a goldfish bowl.

18: Ferah

Falling back was often uncomfortable. The thick history of people was suffocating but the scenery followed visible patterns, near to each other as subways beneath crowded city streets. This time, however, it was like an angry sea. I watched the translucent image of four middle-aged men playing cards tip and sink like a ship. Images impaled the surface of other images before and after us as though someone meant to churn the waters by dropping events like boulders in an ocean. Cars streamed harmlessly through living room windows and whale-sized pieces of earth rolled like disassembled mountains through skyscrapers. I passed through the floor of a cathedral, so much translucent activity collected in one space over the centuries it was a tidy peaceful sun. Passing through, I could barely discern individual actions or anything in the larger world but felt briefly comforted by its glow.

Maddy cried, "Oh, no," as one by one we took notice of Fernando lying lifeless on the ground. It looked as though he'd fallen from a rooftop. He didn't look much older. It seemed impossible all his energy could come to a stop and strange that we'd suddenly see him in a collision of past and future. I don't know what scent brought him to us or if we were brought to him. Still in shock, we saw him alive again, sitting in a café speaking to a woman who said something about the need for a monument to the unlucky: the girl with angry parents, the uncreative life or a man killed by a piano. The outside wall, booth and occasionally shimmering glass crawled by us as Fernando sat back and contemplated the idea. We cried out and waved but he couldn't see us. Finally he said, "People are unlucky to go to war, and almost every city has a war monument." I cried out his name and Fernando seemed to hear me. He looked out the window, though not at me and then he passed, sliding from view behind drifting fields, people and trucks that swept over him like an avalanche.

Oliver wasn't far from me and I knew the others wouldn't be far from him. I saw his anguished look after Fernando was lost from view, and then his attention seemed to catch on something else. The warmth of a summer day came over us, as sudden as someone turning on a light. A mother and a boy sat in a bright, orange car on tracks that was lining up to burst through swinging doors on a ride. She looked down at him and said, "Isn't this fun? Aren't we lucky?" As they were covered in a flurry of activity Oliver turned to me to say that was him, that he was the boy. What sort of ride was beyond the swinging doors? Pirates? A trip to the future? It didn't matter. What mattered was that he carried gratefulness with him and has never forgotten. He said, "We lost her when I was a year out of university."

Perhaps it was only that parents were on my mind but in the chaos I thought I saw my father's thin frame and dark hair. He was a generous soul as well. As a child I had a book on animals with a colour photo of whales that took up a two-page spread in the centre of the book. When I asked to see whales, he seemed to acknowledge and forget, but the following year details of a family vacation began to emerge—we'd go to see whales off the coast of Costa Rica. The lurch and hum of the boat unsettled my stomach and I was sick over the side, finding he and mother had drifted a discreet distance away. They were close enough to help but not close enough to make me feel watched or embarrassed. I was drinking water and feeling better when my father said, "Look, Ferah," and I turned to see a handful of whales surfacing like a new set of slim islands. It was as though they bumped aside the old me and replaced me with someone else, someone with the faith that it was a strange and beautiful world as long as you could see a creature with a heart as big as a car.

My father died the following year and I've always felt his loss. Maybe I only thought of him because I happened to turn my head the same way I did when I looked at the whales. Maybe enough whale-sized objects had sailed around us that it helped me think of that day. Maybe I caught a glimpse of him, distantly busy among the images. But my feelings welled up in me and a spontaneous moment arrived. I trusted my instincts and turned away from my friends toward the image of my father. It was all that was required to lose them in the chaos and I glanced back to see them carry on. I wasn't sure I would see them again, but in any case, something in me was concluded—a quiet pain and a need to search was turned off like a tap.

19: Oliver

THE MADNESS AND CONFUSION CAME TO A SUDDEN end. I saw Catherine again, standing on the grounds of her home before a confused look crossed my face. I collapsed to my knees and unconsciousness took me in its cloak. For a day, I was not aware everyone else had collapsed all around me, nor was I certain we'd lost Ferah. We sat around the comfort of the kitchen table drinking tea beneath the gaze of Catherine's calm green eyes. I had only two friends remaining: Maddy and Aldman. Catherine asked if any of us saw how we'd lost our friend, and Maddy said, "I saw her body turn away from us." There was a pause and it was left to each of us to try to determine why.

"And how did we find ourselves back here?" I asked, but I already sensed the answer. Aldman shifted in his seat and said that with the amount of chaos introduced, "All bets are off, as you say in North America." We decided the last fall through time had been so hectic that exiting it, we'd somehow snapped back to our starting point. Quietly, Catherine closed her eyes and lowered her head a little, her long red hair falling forward to frame her face. It took me a moment to notice, and then I asked her if she was all right. She didn't move but after a long moment lifted her head and I saw it was someone else. I don't mean she had a different face, but it was clear someone else occupied it. There was a new, cautious look behind the eyes and it was as though all the muscles in her face were held differently. She opened her mouth to speak and I knew it to be Athena. "Good to see you, Oliver," she said.

I sat astonished. She seemed awkward, learning a new mouth and stopping to run her tongue along the teeth. A smile spread across her face, slow as a cloud, but as it faded it became clear she had something important to tell me. "Oliver, you've offended a powerful man," she began.

I learned it was someone she called Dr. Waters who caused the disruption we experienced, and that it was his son we injured. The chaos was meant to destroy us and he knew it had failed. As far as she could tell, his new plan was to engineer a specific situation, something outside our reality, involving creatures called Sirens. She didn't know what they would look like or sound like but they'd be designed to draw us away from each other. Alone, there was a stronger possibility we could be killed or thrown somewhere inhospitable.

Athena thought our next fall back would be rushed to us more quickly than we expected but that we could at least prepare for it, securing ourselves in some way before we fell and blocking the sound from our ears. I said that I wanted to hear these creatures and a new smile crossed her face. "Ever-curious Oliver," she said, adding that the others must be able to hold me back if I'm not immune. Then she closed her eyes, lowered her head and returned Catherine to herself.

We took the time to enjoy a meal with Catherine and try to calm our nerves. I was quiet through the meal and told my remaining friends I was sorry for having dragged them into this. They were gracious about it, saying it had been a wild experience. Catherine didn't seem to remember or believe Athena had spoken through her body and shook her head at the idea.

Catherine worked with us. She had no earplugs but expected they would not be sufficient anyway. Her staff arranged for soft, melted wax to be available for us to put in our ears. I refused the wax but sat in the middle of a row of chairs tightly secured to each other by white sheets torn from the beds upstairs. I was bound to my chair with Maddy and Aldman on either side of me. The idea was that we'd move safely through this new challenge together and if I demanded to be released and struggled, my friends were to secure me. We sat and waited.

Waters was not patient. When the first signs we'd fall back arrived, it felt like people brushing by us in all directions though we could see no one. We were sailing together through a valley with cliff walls on both sides though they looked false and constructed in subtle ways, as though the appearance was correct but not all the details were available—a painting half-finished. We had little time to concentrate on the landscape because our attention was caught by two figures on ridges that jutted out from different sides of the valley. One was a black-and-white image of a man in dark suit pants and a dress jacket, like a picture torn from a magazine. On the other side, a woman flared in various colours, complete with an umbrella that blurred more colour into the air behind her. I could see all of us were looking back and forth between them. They were pleasant-looking and I instinctively opened my senses to them. When their mouths opened it was to let out an unbearable noise: the sound of hornets, the wail of alarms, the steady beat of music announcing news.

I writhed in my chair. It was horrific and compelling: I wanted more even as I wanted to tear loose and dive from the chair into the vague mist of events below, just to get away from it. I didn't care that it meant losing my friends, as long as I was away from the overwhelming hold it had on me. Following instructions, the good and reliable Maddy and Aldman worked swiftly to secure me further to my seat. We made our way through the valley this way, with me struggling at the centre like the heart of a wounded bird.

20: Oliver

THE SUDDEN BRIGHTNESS WAS LIKE A SWATH OF OR-
ange daggers. I covered my face with my arm. As my eyes
began to adjust, I saw that we rose and spun as a group.
My mind reeled at the idea we were floating in an orbit
much closer to the sun. Waters had placed a trap within
a trap, and though most of the heat and light was somehow displaced, it was enough that our poorly constructed
carriage of chairs was torn apart, small flames appearing
on the wood to briefly dance and flicker out, vile and
unwelcome.

Once broken apart, my friends and I fell from each
other like groping, failing swimmers. I watched them re-
cede into the distance. The sun was like a living thing, a
god. Incredible tendrils of flame that would dwarf the
Earth erupted from the surface and sailed upwards. Closer to us, I watched a smaller one envelop Aldman and
then Maddy. I writhed in an attempt to turn away from
the scene and saw other solar flares rearing from the surface. I fell unconscious and dreamed of Waters facing my

friends one at a time and lifting his hands to open small rivers of time that surrounded them, changing them and taking them from me.

Reluctantly, I gathered myself into consciousness, aware of a chirping bird and muted sunlight lying across my face, a mask of warmth. I was on my back across the grass and there were teeth coming out of the ground. I was in a mouth. No, there were tombstones on both sides of me. An ache along my entire body made me long to retreat into unconsciousness but I slowly lifted a hand to shield my eyes. Pulling myself to my feet, I caught a glimpse of a woman as she moved between two larger headstones nearby. As I approached, she lifted a camera from around her neck and took a picture that included the top of a small statue, the clouds above and the reaching branches of a tree.

"Hello," I said, having waited a few seconds for her to finish. It didn't interest me to startle her. She looked at me, paused and replied, "You're very calm for a man who looks like hell." I looked down at myself. My hands were pale, paper cutouts. Corners and edges of my clothing had burned off, but the fire had been suffocated when I fell to this place. There was no way to know if it was a lucky accident or if Waters wanted me to carry on without my friends, but the realization they were gone struck me. I put out a hand to a nearby tombstone to steady myself. I looked at an inscription in cold grey along the side of it—*We can all be changed in a moment, in the twinkling of an eye, at the last trump*—and then pitched over into unconsciousness.

I woke in the little cloud of a hospital bed, tucked into white sheets. To my surprise, the woman was there, sitting in an uncomfortable-looking wooden chair. She smiled a little and said, "You're looking better than you did, though I'm afraid that isn't saying a great deal." She was a petite woman, alert and confident. Even sitting in a chair she seemed capable of instant movement as she looked at me. Her short black hair was perfectly in place, neatly framing her face. I couldn't think of anything to say except to ask her name and she gave it: "Calandra." And then I thought to ask her the year, and though she raised an eyebrow she calmly informed me it was the year 2000.

There isn't an easy way to explain why she let me stay in her spare room while I'd recovered a little. Maybe I seemed convincing when I said I had no one. Maybe my most useful skill in life has always been keeping awkwardness to a minimum. She worked a lot as a nurse but on her days off we explored the city, which was a city with a good personality. Glasgow was elusive. It asked you to live there and discover what it offered. I was pleased with the red double-decker buses, black British cabs and everybody driving on the wrong side of the road. A woman had the longest red hair that I'd ever seen. It moved like water in the air.

The St. Mungo Museum of Religious Life and Art presented facts, beliefs and rituals from all the world's major religions, drawing the occasional parallel between them. It would prevent hatred if everyone in the world were to file through the place. I wrote down the description of the Christian faith because I thought it was the most pleasing way I've ever seen it written: *By remembering and reliving Jesus' experiences, believers are reminded of their spiritual debt to God and their responsibilities toward fellow human beings.*

Nearby Glasgow Cathedral dates back to the thirteenth century, complete with oak doors and leaden bullet holes. Behind, in a Victorian cemetery, a statue of Protestant reformer John Knox overlooks the city. Already my old life had started to feel like a recurring dream I'd known and I felt I could stay here. I gradually became aware that I didn't feel the slightest sensation I'd be falling back anytime soon, as though the ability to do it had been stripped from me like a cloak. I had no idea it was something I could possibly miss.

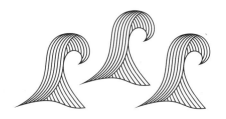

Book Two

21: Calandra

OLIVER INTRIGUED ME, AND FELT RIGHT. HE FIT smoothly into the foreground like a final puzzle piece, something I didn't know I'd been missing. The idea of love at first sight should be replaced with the idea of perfect placement. It was a time of transition for me. A man named Michael had been my focus for about a year, but recently we'd been in a car accident and everything was derailed, literally and figuratively. I was fine but he was hospitalized for contusions and strangely, two broken wrists. As I happened to work as a nurse, I looked in on him often, but I was frequently tired and closely supervised by people who didn't want me to give him any preferential treatment. After he was released, he said he'd had plenty of time to think. He said we'd failed somehow, that we'd grown apart, and that I had been "clinical." Someone who ruins a dream always leaves you with a word like a pin for a balloon.

When your car is struck by another car, everything flies in the air like you're in space. Michael was discharged and asked for exactly that—he asked for space. I let him go. The place two people make together should not be a citadel. It's funny, when two people have a tender first moment on the street, a first kiss, the other people passing them know it can lead to so much potential for misery: days of crying, someone moving out, photos coming down off the walls. The people passing would only need to blurt something out to ruin the moment, but no one does.

Oliver became the man who would leave the hospital and walk into my arms, exactly as Michael should have done. Leaving the hospital, Oliver stood at the top of the steps outside where he looked around and almost seemed to smell the air. It was somewhat infectious the way he treated the air like the sea, as though it could carry you. We drifted around Glasgow for a few days while I took a leave of absence from work and packed my things. It was a three-hour bus ride to Oban with a young couple in front of us, occasionally kissing as though there were no one else in the world. Across from them on the other side of the aisle sat an old couple, calmly affectionate.

Oliver seemed hesitant to touch me. The old couple got off the bus early and the woman turned and waved to the driver. Oban was beautiful and built C-shaped around a small harbour. I always relax in a place that doesn't feel compelled to build higher than a few storeys. We found a hostel painted in bright colours run by a pleasant older man named Jeremy who made a variety of jams for the kitchen, and Oliver asked for two rooms. It shouldn't have surprised me, and yet it did.

We walked the streets of Oban where a wedding party in kilts lined up for a bank machine and seagulls perched around the bay as though they ran the city before they finally dropped off and sailed away. From his window at night I stood with him to watch young Scottish men sing drunken songs as they passed along the street, and I said good night with the feeling we were growing closer. He kept eye contact with me longer and placed a hand on mine as we stood smiling slightly at brave, foolish youth.

Oban also has McCaig's Tower up on the hill: built at the end of the nineteenth century, it was intended to be an art gallery but someone ran out of money and the incomplete structure looks like a broken colosseum. Packages of Walkers Crisps were running an advertising campaign that sort of baffled Oliver: *Win free books for your school!* It wasn't so much that it was a bad idea; he simply said, "I can't imagine a North American product aiming such a campaign at kids." We quietly laughed at an actual item in an Oban convenience store called Inflatable Bonking Sheep (adults only). A small box covered in dust touted a photo of inflatable, excited sheep, an X for each eye, and the tag line, "It will bring out the beast in you."

And then something struck Oliver—perhaps it was his weakened condition—but a cold and fever combination had me returning to his room to check on him and nap lightly beside him, waking once to find his arm over me. We stayed seven nights in Oban, at least partly because of his illness. Weak and slow, he walked with me to the pharmacist to describe his symptoms and the pharmacist smiled and shook his head because he'd recently endured the same thing. Leaving the store, Oliver said, "I admire the kind of people who can smile at little adversities."

Nearby Kerrera was an island with very little on it, but a serious and quiet young local took us and a few others across in a small ferry. All you can do there is walk around or speak to the few locals, but it's a lovely island and we picnicked economically on bread and cheese. Of the many sheep, the adorable younger ones run away and look back, while the completely unimpressed older ones carry on eating. When a fighter jet cracked open the sky above us, Oliver flinched a little. Jeremy later told us they practise around the lochs and islands. I told Oliver, "I'm glad to see you feeling well," as he was lying back on the grass to gaze at the sky. He abruptly sat up to share a long kiss with me.

There are several castles near Oban. We trudged up a steep hill on a hot day to decaying Dunollie with warning signs posted everywhere saying you enter at your own risk. Not a soul there, just the sun burning down on the remains of history. We peed and left. Dunstaffnage Castle nearby had a story to tell—Alexander MacDougall was "foolish" to side with English King Edward the first during the Scottish wars for independence and had his castle just bloody well taken from him by Robert the Bruce in 1309. Imagine: seven hundred years after you die there's a sign posted declaring your foolishness. I looked through stone arrow slits and imagined the attack. The chapel out behind was a pleasant surprise—I expected it to be far less interesting than the castle, but the woods behind were amazingly peaceful: cool and dark, like being underwater with just the occasional pattern of sun on the wood and green mould, the soft bed of dirt and moss. A great fallen tree looked like the visual echo of a woolly mammoth with broken tusk branches.

22: Oliver

MICE ARE A LIVING AFTERTHOUGHT, LIKE THE ECHO
after a symphony. In the darkness, after everything, they
shoot across floors and down corridors, gone by the time
light arrives again. I told Calandra I was tired of feeling like
a mouse. My feelings for my family weren't lost, but events
had been like a series of subtle and persuasive servants
breezing through my thoughts and ushering all remnants
of them to the back rooms of my mind. They weren't *lost* as
much as *displaced*, just as my familiarity with an everyday
world had been taken from me.

We took the wide, white Caledonian MacBrayne ferry
from Oban to Mull, then a jerky bus ride across Mull. It
was uneventful though Calandra pointed out the immense
cloud shadow on the mountain. Then, to a tiny outboard
motorboat that takes tourists to Staffa, an island that looks
like a layered cake. It has simple grassy hills on top, but the
sides of the island have been patiently carved by the sea
into clean line shapes like a great musical organ. Fingal's
Cave is mentioned in a lot of geological textbooks and is

famous for its basalt columns. Mendelssohn was inspired by it when he paid a visit in the summer of 1829. The boat ride was so choppy that we were uncomfortable by the time we got there. Pale and trembling, we reached our final stop of the day: Iona.

A beefy tourist about my own age smiled each time a salty wave hit me until I began glaring at him. When we finally arrived at Iona, we watched him march up the beach with his girlfriend then along the only street while we slowly made our way to the visitor centre to sit and recover over a bowl of soup. Iona has been a centre of religious worship for centuries. Nobody lives on Staffa, but Iona has a road leading from the dock and curving down the length of the island. Calandra loved the multicoloured bricks that were the remains of the nunnery. The larger abbey is still in use, and the small local bookshop had books by residents. Waiting for the Caledonian MacBrayne to take us back to the mainland, we stood on the white sand and watched small streams of water sweep over themselves and fingerpaint in the sand, the darker spots of seaweed showing through the clear green water.

We next made our way to Fort William and found The Lime Tree, an attractive and comfortable lodging run by a local painter and his family. They had travelled the world and decided to settle here in an old house with a lime tree out back. I felt a twinge of jealousy at how contented they seemed. But the answer to jealousy is always to get your own life together, and Calandra and I were delightfully and agonizingly on the edge of some kind of commitment to each other. In the individual rooms, small signs asked people not to smoke and to please respect the home. Sometimes the simplest way to put something is the best. Fort William is an attractive town with parks and one main pedestrian street lined with shops. Occasionally one might notice a slightly odd sign like, *Tim Wynne, family butcher*. We sat by the water and watched trucks move along a nearby landmass like little toys.

Although we could have climbed Ben Nevis, we chose instead to walk along Glen Nevis, a lengthy hike into the open highlands, fields and cliffs. We spotted a few people scaling cliffs without ropes, moving like snails across the great bulging surfaces. I was a little thrown off by the size and horns of ten shaggy brown highland cows. I was more alarmed than Calandra, who just wanted a decent photo of them. I kept bumping her with my hip and saying, "We're getting off to the side!" One of them was curious enough to wander over to the edge of the road, stop and take a long look.

The first time I made love with Calandra was an awakening. This was what it felt like to simply be living your life, weary from a hike but so interested in someone you're willing to tumble into a small mountain range of pillows and sheets with them. As we kissed and tugged at each other's clothing, I paused in the semi-darkness, held myself above her and watched her for a few seconds. The memories of my wife and son were suspended somewhere above me, quietly looking into this world from another, a particular set of dull stars.

23: Calandra

I SOMETIMES BELIEVE PEOPLE SAYING GOOD MORNING all over the world is what makes it a good morning, as though saying the words puts the stitching in the idea, gives it strength and a reality inflatable as a sail. In the morning, we dozed for hours, our bodies calm and sometimes comfortably draped across each other, as welcome and natural as the smell of fresh bread. I recalled a dream that involved a tiny, perceptive person lodged inside my chest behind the sternum. Not really a man or a woman, it had a jellyfish-soft body and was tuned to the number of times I'd do something, including the number of times I'd wake up with a particular lover. It cried out the numbers as best it could, but the voice didn't often reach me through all the tissue and bone. I was giving myself answers and ignoring them.

At one point I watched Oliver sleeping. He had subtle qualities about him that suggested strength, like his thick eyebrows and wide brow. It was strange to be with someone new already, and yet I felt we hadn't rushed anything. As a couple we were wounded.

He said, perfectly, "Good morning," and after breakfast we were on a bus to Portree, spotting the cotton arm of a cloud placed casually around the top of a mountain. Portree was a small town on the Isle of Skye and was a good base for day trips around the island, including Dunvegan Castle, where there is an ancient silk flag that predates the crusades so the locals have no explanation for it except to say that fairies brought it. In a video, current Clan Macleod leader John Macleod takes "fairy power" reasonably seriously, though we didn't suppose there was much choice in the matter. Some stories have it that unfurling this flag brought immense victory and family members carried photographs of it into the First World War. The gardens around Dunvegan were amazing: waterfalls, rock paths, steps and bridges, a bush that burst out into winding moss-covered branches like the varied arms of a small god. Certain paths even had branch walls complete with roof. We spotted rabbits and watched beetles move like little tanks in the dirt.

Walking around Portree, I noted an audience of bluebells on a short hill. We stopped to watch gulls glide and land around circular fishing nets writhing with live meat. Walking away from the sea, the sound of the gulls blended with the sound of the sheep. Our walk took us along the coast and then back around, complete with a dead end we only saw after climbing a steep hill. At one point we climbed a fence wondering if we were trespassing and some farmer was about to start shooting.

As we sat on a bench I heard a bird behind me and

turned to see it braced perfectly against the wind, holding in the air and singing. I knew it would only last a matter of seconds and elbowed Oliver to look but he was mostly annoyed at my way of getting his attention and by the time he turned his head, that little glass moment had broken and the bird shot away through the air, which left me feeling more or less alone in the world.

We stayed at a half-finished but clean hostel where an American named John told us his travel stories, even while acknowledging that it was "about time" for him to be heading home to start a family. The only way to speak was to attempt to interrupt, which wouldn't slow him down at all, but he'd eventually ask, "What were you going to say?" He was a nice man and had been all over, but his accent and tone could make the name of a foreign city sound like a swear word. Our window overlooked the water and when we returned at night it was a sheet of perfectly still blue glass holding the ships, two misty arms of land out to sea on both sides.

Portree also had the An Tuireann Arts Centre, where I found a book of Scottish haiku at its bookstore. On our last day we visited "the Lump," the oddly situated point in town where they have highland games, though none were happening. It's almost a cliff edge, but with a circular space for the games. Some of the trees have been shaped by the wind and the crows among the trees were a constant presence as we walked up the path. I sensed some kind of measured and meaningful echo should emerge from all that activity in one place, but nothing did.

24: Oliver

"NOT, I THINK, TODAY," REPLIED THE EMPLOYEE AS A decent-condition paperback was pushed across the counter back at me. Somehow, being surrounded by wall-to-wall books in a historic building with a second-floor café on a balcony gives the impression everyone will be relaxed and pleasant. I understood it was awkwardness, a certain shyness from the employee. If you've been around the block enough times, your antennae picks that up. Really, my mood was hurt by a feeling of guilt acting as a heavy poison in the mind. I didn't immediately feel I'd betrayed anyone, as this felt like a whole new life, but the idea was obviously there, below the surface, quiet as an eel. It was only a twinge of feeling as we'd arrived in Inverness and wandered into the bookstore, but it was certainly there.

Next, we stood in Culloden Battlefield, a poor choice for Bonnie Prince Charlie and the Clansmen to battle government troops in his attempt to take over the throne. One of their advantages was the alarming reputation of the fierce highland charge, and yet they chose to meet on a field full of heather. I tried to imagine myself falling back to it. The government troops slaughtered hundreds of wounded men in these fields, believing the propaganda that their own wounded would have been shown no mercy. An easy lie, a small seed of anger dropped in all of their minds. I imagined myself arriving with a shockwave before the armies clashed, like a boulder in the centre of a puddle, forcing them all to retreat.

Still feeling dispirited, I went with Calandra the next day to Drumnadrochit near Loch Ness, where a sign suggested a man sold "nessie-cery" models of Nessie to finance his full-time monster search from a trailer near the Loch. I put a finger in the edge of the great, dark Loch Ness and touched the water, imagining this small intrusion was somehow sensed by the creature. "It's cold," I said, looking up at Calandra. Nearby Urquhart Castle is mostly a ruin though you can still climb the tower and descend into the basement. A piper played on the castle wall in a drizzle of rain and the view across the loch, through the mist and grey of the day, looked like a black-and-white photo. "I like the idea something's out there," Calandra said.

My preoccupation with history continued. On some level I thought standing around in historical settings might allow for some connection to a greater pattern, an understanding of our future. Of course I knew the future, generally speaking, but I wanted to know about my own personal future, and still thought of Penelope and Tomas. We visited the Clava Cairns, rock pile tombs dating back to three or four thousand BC. Today they're roofless, so you walk into them down a tunnel and step into a round central area, the upper half only clear, blue sky. Trees with drooping branches were scattered around the clearing and Calandra said, "It's like they're slowly moving onto a dance floor." One small part of me, like one voice at the back of a crowded room, felt the weight of all this history and longed for the future I'd lost. Where were they, my wife and son?

25: Calandra

"I'm fine," he said, but Oliver seemed to be struggling with something. He was pleasant, but also languid and hesitant as we took a bus, a ferry and another bus to Kirkwall on the Orkney Islands. It was about as far north as you could go in Scotland and Kirkwall was a strange, cold town, at least upon first impression. Every grey, concrete building was the same colour as the sky above. We saw a young man running at older, slower tourists and then turning away at the last moment. Oliver started toward him but I took his arm, told him, "Leave it," and pulled him away with me.

We assumed maybe the bus hadn't let us off at the station so we asked someone where the station was. A thin man simply gestured back at the parking lot, burst out laughing and carried on his way. The hostel was an official international youth hostel where they hand you sheets and you walk a long hallway to a clean, cold bunk. You couldn't help but think of a prison. They lock you out between ten and five during the day and lock up again at midnight.

But Kirkwall also had St. Magnus Cathedral, eight hundred years old, built of red sandstone and quite beautiful. Some tombstones only sigh and say, *Thy will be done*, but the ones in the interior walls talked about "cruel fate" and always ended with *Memento Mori*, or sometimes with a skull and crossbones or an hourglass. We stopped to look at it for long minutes before Oliver said, "I think a cathedral as old as that would feel the people only a little more than it would feel the wind."

Local folklore was fascinating: a few signs posted around the cathedral were enough to tell us that people used to believe large stones had powers and were sites to make marriage vows; that some stones must go to the loch to drink a few times a year; and that an agreement made at the tomb of Bishop Thomas Tulloch was as good as a binding legal contract. Walking back into town we witnessed a "blackening" where the locals about to be in a marriage party get harmless, sticky black goo smeared all over them, then drive around making a lot of noise, banging and yelling from the back of a pickup. "At least wave, damn you," I said to Oliver, and we put our hands high in the air.

Skara Brae provided a demonstration of some parts of history surviving even as others are wiped away: homes of piled stone and earth dug slightly into the ground dated back to 3100 BC, though the roofing materials weren't as lasting and have since vanished. But how mesmerizing to stand in those spaces and think it was someone's home at such a distant time. It's a similar feeling to one I had at the Clava Cairns but remarkably, the stone shelves at Skara Brae have survived.

We were both deeply irritated to see modern graffiti at the Ring of Brodgar, where twenty-seven flat stones still stand out of an original sixty. Nobody is sure of its original purpose exactly, but it was likely a religious centre. When we reached the burial chamber of Maeshowe, I didn't expect much. It looked like a hill with an entrance, hollow and made of great stone slabs. Our slow-talking guide with a bushy beard trained his flashlight on much older graffiti left in the form of runes by Vikings in the twelfth century. The scrawl, *Ingigerth is the most beautiful of all women*, was next to the image of a slavering dog.

I'd always been interested in graffiti but was suddenly struck by the idea of it as a mental photograph, a brief note for all time, either insightful or completely daft depending on the person and the moment. I pictured people fluttering the way they do in time-lapse photography, leaving the world a work of art or a daughter, cups and bowls used and replaced in flashes from the stone shelves at Skara Brae. What else do people leave? There must be more existing as hidden currents and repercussions. We went to the Italian Chapel built by Italian prisoners of war from a standard building. They painted walls to look like ornate brick and made lanterns from beef tins.

As Oliver stood looking around I decided I should let things take their course. It's possible it wasn't meant to happen for us, difficult as that might be to accept. Or maybe it wasn't meant to *last*. Some islanders used to get mail to the mainland simply by sealing it up and dropping it in the water, trusting it to the currents. If something is meant to happen, the currents take care of it.

26: Oliver

In Arbroath we stayed at a bed and breakfast, though it was really just a small home run by an elderly Mrs. Brooks and her husband. He was a plume of white hair embedded in the couch in front of the TV. He didn't speak or look at us except to wave when we arrived. Mrs. Brooks' eyes were magnified by her bottle-thick glasses into tremendous fluttering moths. She warmly collected our bags and we went out to the main street. The town was a coastal fishing community with a harbour that extended walls of stone around a collection of boats like protective arms. Offshore, the Bell Rock Lighthouse sat on a reef twelve feet underwater at high tide. Construction required stopping work to jump on ships after a design was worked out by Robert Stevenson, grandfather of Robert Louis Stevenson. The signal tower on shore could be seen raising a pair of trousers if the lighthouse keeper became the father of a boy, or possibly a little dress.

Calandra wanted to walk around the harbour, moving from one plaque to another, and watch the locals. We stopped to eat an "Arbroath Smokie"—haddock smoked over oak chips—and read about gale winds taking apart the harbour in 1706. There were impressive waves right at that moment, pounding and breaking on the walls, and a handful of children ignored yellow warning signs about the risks of getting too close in favour of cycling over patches of seaweed and puddles, creating brief, muddy fins of water.

Maybe the slightly urgent feeling of the harbour helped it along, but I felt a slow and growing alarm, a need to make something work and not simply be buffeted around by the tides, clinging to old memories like a collection of trinkets. I could insist on at least one thing: Calandra as a living life-boat of experience. She could become all I keep and all I need. I went over to her and pressed our hands together, pulling her away from the harbour.

Hand in hand we walked to the Arbroath Abbey, over eight hundred years old and sandstone the colour of a dull red bushel of apples. I'd long known Arbroath was in my family background so we went to a local records centre outside an office with a frosted-glass shutter that closed off a desk space in the wall. We'd failed to notice a sign that advised we ring the buzzer for service, but it didn't matter as the dark, blurred outline of a man emerged, paused, and came toward us to lift the window. He was a slim, middle-aged man and greeted us simply and pleasantly. I liked him immediately.

We walked through the local cemetery with a map to the grave of my great-great-grandfather, which certainly gave me an odd feeling on a bright summer day. The stone declared him a cabinetmaker and listed his wife Annie and all the various children, many of them young when they died. I'd been told he started a combination furniture store and undertaker business, which strikes me as curious, but if you're good at making things, why not include coffins? I can recall one of his sons, Alexander, was told to stop drinking the profits and took such offence that he packed up his family and began a new life in Canada. I realized I knew only this much as I put a hand on aging stone and marvelled at how little it revealed.

On our final day in Arbroath we decided to explore the Devil's Head. On our way, a soccer ball bounced toward us and I threw it back to perfectly still, strangely tense boys who didn't trouble themselves to say thanks. It made me worry that kindness was an oddity here, but perhaps they were just unaccustomed to seeing strangers in such a small town. Fortunately, I had a far stronger memory of Mrs. Brooks as we checked out of her tiny home. Her traditional British breakfasts—meat and more meat, fried tomatoes—had been a challenge for Calandra and her stomach, but saying farewell to us, she came out to teeter on her front steps, blink her magnified eyes and waved repeatedly as she called out, "All the best, all the best!"

27: Calandra

"It's possible Robert Burns deserves better than having a sketch of his face over a steaming cup of coffee outside a gift shop and café," Oliver said. "And it's possible he'd have simply laughed," I replied. In Ayr we'd seen the Robert Burns cottage, museum, monument and gardens, but had drawn the line at some kind of production called "The Tam O'Shanter Experience." Oliver said it was the only thing even approaching bad taste, and he appeared to be settling into and enjoying Scotland and its people.

We'd been to the Island of Arran for an impressive local music festival in Lochranza where the bus barrelled along the single road, and Oliver noted a packed group of riders enduring the experience by laughing uproariously as they were thrown around. On the way home, a skinny drunk man stood above Oliver with a cup of beer and Oliver turned to me as if to say, *I'm going to have beer spilled on me.* When the splatter of beer landed on his leather jacket, the man apologized and promptly licked it off. My favourite moment of the night, however, was the lights of the bus receding into the absolute darkness of the island; a set of Christmas lights on the wind as we stood with our hands locked together.

As I lay with Oliver that night, I felt I had him and was with him, but couldn't progress into his life. I could never meet his uncle or a former girlfriend. It wasn't possible to run into someone on the street and have it trigger an old memory or story. I asked him about his childhood and there was a long pause until he finally said, "People think Canada is all snow but as a child the summer months would roll by like slow, iron railcars hot to the touch. June, July and August." To name them ends them, but when he was a very young child they weren't named. In the fall everything crumbled beautifully and then winter arrived to cover the world in sheets of snow, sometimes several feet deep, as though to offer the landscape a fresh start. At that time, Canada had it all and people didn't even know it.

Oliver said he felt most safe sleeping in the backseat of the car on the way home with his parents in the front and the waterfall sound of passing cars accompanying his sleep. There's a certain irony in feeling safest on the road, but I told him I'd felt the same way nodding off on the route between Glasgow and Edinburgh, even though the trip took under an hour. A public servant and a professional arts organizer, my parents took pride in taking me to cultural events, particularly Edinburgh in August when all the festivals were happening and the population nearly doubled. My mother could organize an interesting, well-attended lecture and even show up with two pies to add to the food table.

As always, I stayed with Oliver for a few days somewhere and we began to feel the need to go somewhere else. I started to think of Edinburgh as somewhere we might settle a while. It wouldn't be my home city and we might make a fresh start there together. I thought we might find the right balance: sometimes the earth is too tight a net and I toss and worry, feel the heavy shift of everything, of too much at once. At other times the net is too loose and it's as though I'm ungrounded, slipping away in the current of a river. I wanted Oliver, a new life and balance.

28: Oliver

WE ALL KNOW THE BASIC LANDSCAPE OF MEMORY: SO much recedes into the background while other events, sometimes even meaningless ones, stand out like mountain ranges, winning out and becoming part of our identity simply because they survive. My greater sense is the sense of time lost, and yet I'm glad to own what I distinctly remember as it's all I have.

I told Calandra about our family driving every summer to visit my grandparents in St. Stephen, New Brunswick. Three children in the backseat trying not to complain of boredom or frustration, particularly as their mother was like some kind of magician, reaching down to produce a new book or toy whenever we did break down and complain. When we drove thirteen hours once, it was our mother who broke down suddenly, crying, "Thirteen hours!" Our father went from oblivious to startled, and within fifteen minutes had checked us into the first clean motel that came along. She'd been making polite comments that were ignored or brushed off. We all took our father's support for granted, wolfing down hamburgers on the road and checking into rooms as simply the next thing, and the next.

We stayed in a boldly painted green cottage that my grandparents owned—I can still hear the creak and clap of the screen door, see the handmade green steps down the cliff's edge that took you to the beach and the slightly wobbly branch nailed up on two posts for a handrail. Digging for clams, building a fort on the beach with my brother because a pirate invasion was coming, sitting on the little screened-in front porch that never seemed small: it was perfect and it was enough. The year I was there for the last time I sat on a large rock that would be surrounded by the sea when the tide came in, and silently declared it mine, though of course I never returned. It wasn't until years later my mother told me they weren't necessarily pleased to go every summer, but that my grandparents expected it.

But none of that matters now. Our bus carried us into the remarkable city of Edinburgh, and as we began to walk the streets, those memories only mattered as an exchange, as something that allowed us to feel closer and a reminder to be careful about our rituals. Edinburgh had statues everywhere, it seemed. We saw Greyfriars Kirkyard, a very old graveyard and home to John Gray and Bobby, his dog. John died in the nineteenth century and his dog reportedly slept on his grave for at least fourteen years. When the dog finally died, it was decided he deserved to be given a place of honour with his master, and there's a small statue where the dog lays as well. Perhaps some rituals shouldn't be questioned.

We walked up the winding, spiral stairs of the Scott Monument, dedicated to Sir Walter Scott. The wind and cramped spaces almost goaded us on and discouraged us at the same time. It stands out on Princess Street like a cross between a ceremonial dagger and a layered cake. Stopping on the four levels, you see how imagination was made physical with tiny statues of Scott's fictional characters all the way up. As the wind slapped at my legs, I imagined it was the hand of one of those characters.

It's an impressive view, but we soon longed for something more relaxing and found our way to a bench in the park, listening to the wind sing through the openings of our beer bottles. I felt a tap on top of my head and turned around to look back after a small roar of laughter could be heard.

"Nice one, mate!" A boy gave the thumbs up and grinned wickedly as a group began to spill away. One of them had tossed a crumpled paper ball so it hit me on the top of my head. The anger trickled into me like fuel and ignited itself but I checked my impulse to get up and chase them. They'd only scatter like mice. "Bastards," I said, but Calandra retorted, "They're just boys." "Yeah, but what else do they get up to?" I said.

We sat for a long while, and later one of the boys came running along with a tall man after him. The boy was about to run right by me and would've been surprised if I suddenly grabbed him. I had a decision to make, and a second to make it. I did nothing. The boy raced by us and around the bench, easily eluding the man who gave up and came to a stop. A dishevelled older woman ambled over to us, slow as a plump cloud. I thought she was coming very close for someone who wanted to pass us, but then she sat down on our bench and asked for some of our baguette. "Of course," Calandra said before tearing off a piece.

"It's lovely bread; it melts in your mouth," the woman said quietly before asking, "Could I have a little more?" We all sat comfortably a while and agreed with her on the immortal Scottish saying, "It's a wee bit nippy out." Even as you're a joke to one person, you're an angel to someone else.

29: Calandra

I WOKE IN THE MIDDLE OF THE NIGHT WHEN I FELT the hideous tickle of an insect on my body and sat upright, instantly awake and flailing about like someone lost at sea, desperate to get the small creature off me. We'd stayed for a few nights at a hostel that put up to six people in a room, and I'd noticed the bugs before. Perhaps my body was sensitively waiting for the moment one of them found me. Our money was starting to run low and we walked Princess Street to find a coffee shop and sat griping at each other miserably. We answered ads, making calls through the morning to see if we could arrange somewhere to stay, though we'd also need to find work quickly and I felt that pressure constantly. As we made calls at a payphone I held the coins and tried not to think of them as our hope draining away.

An art student named Alan sounded calm and reasonable through the receiver. We made an arrangement to meet but he wasn't free until around four so we had most of the day to ourselves. "This way," Oliver said, and as I suspected, he led me to the Museum of Childhood. He'd mentioned he wanted to see it and even if we had concerns about money, I thought it might lift our spirits. I stared for at least a few minutes at a shoe doll made for a girl in a poor family: a cloth dress wrapped around a shoe, the face made from tape on the bottom of the heel. I wanted the story of the person who made it to come out of the face, but the story refused to appear except to state the obvious: it was about sadness and about love. The first school uniforms, it would seem, were for schools founded by charitable organizations that ensured proper clothing and reminded children they were objects of charity. In a so-called horror box, a penny in a slot brought a small, carefully crafted house to life: a painting lit up, a man in a chair lifted his newspaper as if he heard a noise, a square-headed monster came partway through the door.

Walking to meet Alan at his apartment, we carried the same bags we'd always carried but they felt heavy with an anxious feeling, a need to find a home. I tried not to voice it, but I wondered out loud the whole way over if his home would have bugs, leaving us adrift again. "There are no bugs," Oliver said. I could tell he was trying to be patient but that he was becoming increasingly irritated as we reached Bread Street and the heavy black door. We took three floors of stone steps with a regular dip in the middle. Alan was tall, pleasant and calm, with a short mess of brown hair. Immediately I said, "Do you have any bugs?" He looked around nervously, one set of fingers resting on his chin. "Bugs? No, I don't think so."

We had found a home and were grateful for Alan's gentleness, though no home is a perfect one. Oliver was irritated with the fact that there was no shower in the bathroom, only a tub with a short hose attached to the faucet. "What the hell is this?" I heard him whisper to himself. But it was a small, remarkable pleasure to be able to put food in a fridge again and look out the window from the little kitchen on Edinburgh castle.

30: Oliver

WE SETTLED INTO A ROUTINE AND BEGAN POLISHING the stone that made up those slightly slippery steps a little further every day with our coming and going. Calandra found work in an office where polite Scottish men would ask her to get them a coffee, and when she calmly and warmly replied, "I think you can get a coffee for yourself," they'd say, "Oh, right!" I found work in the box office of a nearby theatre which showed independent and foreign films. The staff seemed a typical collection: one quiet man, one endlessly outgoing young man who seemed to transform to meet the needs of different people and a busybody who looked over my shoulder my entire first shift but eventually relaxed somewhat. I'd braced myself for the public to be terse and difficult, but people in Edinburgh were generally calmer and more appreciative than they were in Toronto. I had to tell one person after another we'd have the programs for the Edinburgh Film Festival next week, later than expected, and they all dropped some genuine expression of thanks, or even exclaimed surprisingly, "That's magic."

A few weeks after we'd settled into the city, the local papers proclaimed an accidental death, the result of a section of brickwork breaking loose and falling forty feet where it barrelled through a glass canopy and hit a young man on the head as he served customers on a local patio. He'd apparently worked there for years and was originally from New Zealand. It stayed in my head for days. I felt distaste for the paper and its photo of scattered glass, the attention-grabbing headline about sudden death. But more than anything else, I thought of this man working there for years while brickwork slowly decayed. If he'd quit, called in sick that day or had merely been standing in a different spot, he'd have lived. If he'd never left New Zealand or decided to study somewhere else he'd be alive. But all those things fell into place and he died. Fate is our small word for the unlikely arrival of anything, and people are left forever baffled and angry at a pointless loss. The papers said the ongoing vibration of traffic can slowly unravel old buildings and suggested the whole city needed an overhaul, but I only saw work done on that building.

"We've been here weeks and I still marvel at this place," Calandra said. Edinburgh was like some kind of coherent Escher drawing that worked on various levels, and it continued to amaze me, too. Victoria Terrace runs along Victoria Street and looks down onto another street with a black iron railing running along it. There are narrow alleyways that run between buildings, so there are subtle shortcuts everywhere, some of them opening up to small squares with gardens or benches. The entire central core, or old town, is historical which is simply something we don't have much of in Canada. People seemed to appreciate the value of a pleasant day so much that the whole population came out to Meadows Park whenever the clouds parted and the drizzle was banished.

31: Calandra

We settled into our lives and then it felt as though we turned around and found we had been there nearly a year. Like a person, a city takes time to get to know until it's taken for granted, assumed to be there. And much like a person, it's possible to find out things you'd rather not have known.

Oliver frequented a used bookshop a few doors down from us and though it was a small place, it had enough dim alcoves to allow the feeling that you could get lost in the shelves. The owner was a thin, older man with receding hair and ears that perched like little parachutes on the side of his head. Oliver always chatted happily with him. The owner had a calmness Oliver liked, and said he could tell Canadians from Americans, which certainly pleased Oliver, but he also leaned back with a certain satisfaction when talking, as though he felt it necessary to overcompensate for something. Maybe he felt conscious of being a mere bookstore owner. Oliver didn't believe in this sort of hierarchy anyway.

"My employee is a bit brown, but he could pass for a Paki," the owner said, and Oliver and I both tensed. In Canada, "Paki" was too crude a word, a blanket term for anyone with brown skin. The bookstore owner seemed oblivious to our anxiety. We'd overheard "Paki bastard" on Edinburgh streets a few times and were saddened by it. The city of dreams had a darker underside which, in part, contained the idea that different kinds of employment and treatment waited for those with brown skin.

It reached the point where we could take in Edinburgh and its great, stone history at a glance. We passed the stone toes of statues without looking up. No longer at all startled by our surroundings, we fell into the same mildly focused sleep so many of us know, the quiet and halfway-conscious collecting of moments and items, an idea I became some-what fascinated by. For example, I overheard a woman on a patio say, "Manners are an act of faith." A man has all the food he needs, a warm place to sleep every night, but still demands that a surly grocery clerk be fired. I overheard a man telling a friend, "I need a little music to tell me every-thing's all right." An unbalanced man lectured nobody in particular on a street corner, his hands spidering in the air, little classes of deaf, bubbled people in cars stopping next to him, lining up to look and leave, over and again.

While in nursing school I also worked at a bookstore, and in particular at the information and special orders desk affectionately known as "special odours." Nearly every day an elderly man arrived as regularly as the moon. He had something of a thick accent and was Russian, I think, though I never asked him. He was always buying and ordering books. When I was told to ask him for a deposit on an expensive hardcover, he looked at me with a hard, level gaze and said, "When I order, I buy." We never asked him for another deposit. Slowly, he grew warmer and I grew to recognize his curiosity about the world was the reason for all the book orders. I suspected he couldn't afford to travel much, and travelled instead through books. He would say, "Good morning," and I would say, "Good morning" back. We had his fax number on file and once, accidentally, we sent him our sales reports for the day which he found very amusing.

After that I went to work in the fiction section, or maybe it was around then he simply stopped coming in, I can't remember. But all these years later I suddenly remembered him. He'd be gone now. He was old even then but it occurs to me I was pleased to see him coming and his calm, civil way of doing things. At the time, I didn't even note that I no longer saw him. How could that have happened?

Oliver and I were both wounded but I think we'd found something in each other through circumstance and developed an unexpected generosity with each other. I only worried sometimes that he would someday be as lost to me as an elderly man who'd once greeted me every day as part of his morning ritual. Time is a sniper.

32: Athena

WATERS ASSUMED OLIVER TO BE DEAD, OR LOST AND miserable. Even if the evidence were recorded, there were no established laws for murder to draw on. The death becomes what always happened. Legally it was a new frontier. Sometimes Waters still placed his two hands on the wall on either side of the data ocean and leaned into it looking for Oliver as a submarine officer would stare through a periscope. But we'd lost the thread of his story, and only an unlikely chance would ever allow Waters to find him again. Unlikely but possible. Certainly, Waters never seemed to forget.

I say if you need to track someone, use a dog. I already regret my choice of that particular word because Herman proved to be more real to me each time I resurrected my temporary, living messenger of bundled energy and memories. He was made of wind but smiled when given another chance at life. Perhaps his brief moments were each a lifetime to him. As before, he was assembled from the images and records of a businessman and father of two, but more and more data clung to him as more records and photographs were found. He wore a suit that swam with images: his daughters, his round-faced wife and the long drive of a family vacation. Again, his tall frame, dark eyes and sharp face were striking to me. I felt somewhat guilty at not giving him ongoing life and stood staring at him a moment. In that moment, he surprised me: turning without instruction, he vanished.

Checking on him—for he was designed to be traceable—I saw that he materialized in the morning light of a clear blue sky above Chicago, descending like a superhero next to a brown building with the lattice of a black fire escape down one corner. He walked a few blocks under the elevated subway trains that slip between buildings. Ignoring any startled looks he may have received, he went striding to an intersection on South Michigan Avenue where a plastic and metal canopy over a subway entrance partially blocked drivers' views.

"This is where my heart was closed for business," he said to the air as though a camera was present. He knew I'd be listening. And then his earlier self and his family approached the street corner he stood on, startled and slowed by his presence there, his suit still swimming with images meaningful to him. He went down on both knees as though to make himself into a small roadblock of some kind. He looked at his younger daughter, tried to meet her eyes and held out a hand flat in a motion that said, *Stop*. In clumsily pulling him from history, I'd not looked closely enough at him; I had not seen he was a wounded man.

Herman hadn't done much, but slowing down his family was enough as a car peeled and flashed around the corner where his youngest daughter had been standing before. Perhaps she had gone running ahead excitedly—I confirmed the data even as it melted away and was gone, and could hardly blame him for wanting to correct a world where a child's teeth can be scattered like dice. As he and his family began to find the right words to ask a question, he took a moment to smile and look at them all. He raised himself to his feet, turned away from them and looked up into the air to say, "I am available to you." He was mine again. He'd saved his family, and he was mine again.

33: Herman

"Be happy," was the only trite thing I could think of to say, despite a swelling of emotion upon seeing my family again. I could move somewhere as soon as I think of it, but crawled through language as though through brambles. If I needed to speak it was necessary to think first, and I turned away from my family and even from myself, rather than explain. I said, "I am available to you." I said it into the air and then walked around the corner to vanish to another part of the city. As for my former self, I think he'd have understood there was just too much to explain, which is what I believe they call an understatement.

What I understand now is time. I see different kinds of events, linked and growing together as different species of plants and animals do. It's possible to see if you can only read the signs. While a dendrologist can walk through the woods, notice a sick birch tree and decide to leave the woods, I could not step outside time any more than anyone else.

Athena had given me a great gift. I could go anywhere I wanted to go and she trusted me to honour her request to find Oliver. At first, I foolishly took myself to Toronto, his home, and looked around at the clear blue to be found between downtown skyscrapers. It made little sense to go somewhere he'd already left, but some part of me wanted both my freedom and a half-hearted gesture toward the goal she'd given me. I walked for hours. It was possible for me to see a great deal, and watching a few people put a couch at the side of the road, I was tempted to tell them it was the wrong time to do it. Watching someone walk down the street, alone and huddled into themselves, I knew it was a failing romance, quieter than a paddle in water. I stopped to look around frequently, searching for small rewards.

I followed a woman in her early twenties into a bookstore. She browsed her way through the store, spoke to an employee, her body a polite arrow turned away from me. The books, colourful and arranged across a few tables, also caught my attention but I think she began to sense me, and hating to make anyone uncomfortable, I forced myself to go out the door and onto the street. I'd forgotten my frame was a middle-aged one. It's easy to forget something like that.

The crowd swept me along and I followed the river of bodies down the steps of a subway entrance. This was a mistake for me as I hated crowds and I hated to be underground, lost underneath everything, hidden in the world's engine. I took a random subway train and thought I could see a man displaced in time, clinging to a subway pole. He seemed to sway to his own, different rhythm. The situation was intolerable and I took myself far away, appearing in the upper atmosphere and into a wind-whipping fall before I brought myself to the surface below me, this time in Greece.

It was a busy town square and I sat on the edge of the fountain. In the distance, I saw a girl walking diagonally across the square toward me. Small and frail, she stood out. Her shoulders were sharp squares, her legs delicate and thin in white stockings. She had long, stringy black hair hanging down the back of her pink dress. Despite her youth, she walked with poise and dignity such as I'd never seen before. She glided through the heat and yellow dust of the square. As she came closer to me, I realized she wasn't a little girl at all, but a very elderly woman. She had a story in every line of her over-painted face. I wondered if she was Death or just another person displaced in time, but eventually concluded she was someone bearing the weight of a lifetime on those little, square shoulders. I felt anxious as her path took her past me without so much as a glance my way.

I knew I should be thinking about Oliver and recalled the data Athena had given me. I dragged a few of my fingers through the water in the fountain and looked up again to catch a last glimpse of the old woman as she turned a corner. Vaguely I thought of Oliver and then his elderly relatives. If you cannot find a person, begin by finding a way to the person. I saw an old Scottish woman who had come to Canada at around age nineteen, and then I saw her as a girl in Arbroath with her twin sister. They were sitting on a low, stone wall around a white house by a patch of woods, keeping still in the hope of seeing rabbits. The girl would become his grandmother. I had found a thread. I stood to leave and turn my attention to Scotland.

34: Calandra

I'M NOT SURE WHY HE CAUGHT MY ATTENTION. HE stood on the street corner looking around, tall and calm as a pelican. The mildly alarming thing was that he turned to look at me as though I was the thing he was looking for. The ground seemed to shift as he walked. For a tall man with sharp features, he moved more gracefully than he should have and crossed the street through slowing cars and the sound of horns as if oblivious to them. To my surprise, his sharp features melted into a warm smile that didn't linger long on his face before he stopped in front of me.

"It's time to set him free," he said simply, though of course there was nothing simple about what this meant. I was rattled and took a step back. He gave me his name, "Herman," and smiled again, but how did he know about Oliver? I turned to go, saying, "He is freely living with me," over my shoulder though I immediately sensed it was a mistake to have responded at all.

When I later saw Oliver, I asked, "How was today? Did you find anything?" and winced a little inwardly at having not paused between the two questions. I'd found work as a nurse that usually kept me late, but Oliver was between jobs, and I knew he didn't feel good about it. "No, afraid not," he answered.

Oliver had paused a Western with Jimmy Stewart, and I knew he wanted to turn it on again. We spent an uneasy evening together and I wasn't sure how to approach him about Herman. I thought perhaps Herman would just go away. We made dinner in our little, white kitchen and watched the rest of the Western as though a man interested to introduce a personal earthquake into our lives was not lingering around somewhere just out of sight. It was *The Naked Spur*, among the few Westerns ever nominated for an Academy Award for the screenplay. As a final film to watch together, not bad.

I found it difficult to hate Herman, despite what he represented, probably because of the way he smiled without arrogance. I heard someone once say that hatred is a failure of the imagination, a failure to be able to imagine yourself in someone else's place.

But there was little compensation for the thought of losing Oliver and not even knowing how to approach him about it. Our apartment and our slowly growing collection of things did hum a little more loudly now that I knew it might not last much longer, and so I paid more attention to it, drifting a hand across the spines of the two shelves of books we'd collected so far. Tired, I pressed the same few fingers to my forehead and felt the thin layer of warmth and smoothness that covered my skull. Oliver asked me if something was wrong but I smiled and told him, "No." That night I dreamed again of the jellyfish person lodged in me, able to signal how many more times something could happen. He seemed louder this time, quivering, matching my beating heart, and I woke up in a sweat.

At least it wasn't a gradual loss, but a particularly vivid day brought on by a man in a suit that, now that I think about it, swam with images of people who must've been important to him. I didn't know for sure where he was from but he sounded American. Who needs a passport when your body lives and breathes whatever is important to you?

"A pleasant day to you," Herman said as he passed us, and he kept on down the street. I later caught sight of him crossing the street and a few days later in our favourite place for chips with curry sauce. He was there having a meal in a booth. I noticed the images on his suit had slowed to almost a crawl so that you might only notice that by the time he left, his clothing looked quite different. He didn't look at us and Oliver didn't notice him, but it brought home the inevitability of telling Oliver.

"I think we should have a conversation with that man," I said impulsively and Oliver turned to look at him. There was a pause and to my surprise Oliver said, "We've met." Looking up as though he sensed we were ready, Herman smiled and gestured to the seats opposite him in the booth.

"Athena," he explained, "has found a way for Oliver to live more safely." He spoke without any preamble, and carefully as though he'd practised it. "As it is, Waters engages in casual searches but he'll find you someday. Athena will bring you to the future you lost where Waters will not look for you. And she can disguise the possibility."

Back with Penelope they'd be shielded by a mountain peak of old time over them, showing they weren't together. Everybody had this, of course, but usually it was behind them or ahead of them. After all, even if they stayed together as a couple, people die. Athena said Oliver and Penelope could have whatever amount of time they'd have together and she'd pattern it to look otherwise.

And that was how it ended. Oliver and I had been given a year together and now it was over. I saw my country again and made it his country, at least for a time. We had a first step and with only a small amount of imagination we could see a future together. But nothing is forever. Some things only establish themselves and then leave. In return it can be said we appreciated them all the more. Oliver came to me as dazed as a shipwrecked sailor and I gave him back to the sea.

35: Oliver

I trusted Athena and her mechanical man. It wasn't completely surprising to see him. I'd started to feel something was coming to interrupt our lives, the way a part of you instinctively feels the rain coming on or the light beginning to go. The man's eyebrows worked like a set of dark caterpillars as he explained, "Athena can place you in frozen time, alive, in a cemetery to wait out the long years. You'll sleep through it untouched."

I considered it for a few minutes and admitted, "I guess I like the idea of being alive in the middle of a cemetery, like one flower emerging through a crack in a paved road." Our hard, plastic booth had a large window facing the street. I was able to see an old man stopped outside standing more or less next to us and peering into the window for a long moment, though a glance told me he was only trying to see the menu of fish, chips and pies, and perhaps to see what was scattered below under an orange heat lamp.

Herman looked startled and captivated by the old man's thin face. His eyes were widened slightly in a very human expression of mild alarm. Maybe there was more to the mechanical man. I don't know that it was a conscious decision he made, but the still images on his jacket and vest shifted away and were replaced with Penelope, who seemed to be looking at me. It was my turn to look mildly shocked. I believe Calandra saw it too, and we both knew I couldn't resist returning to the family that rested quietly in my thoughts. Herman brought his attention back to us again and the images changed, turning back to a set of people I assumed to be his family.

"Let's go," Calandra said quietly. He had explained everything while we sat in silence, an increasingly heavy feeling settling over us. I went home with Calandra in that silence, and we went up the stone steps to our apartment painfully aware it might be for the last time. I don't think there's anything harder than going through a last time for everything: a last sleep together in our wide bed, her breathing next to me; a last morning and breakfast. I looked up the information about trains to Arbroath. We had been told this could be done anywhere but I felt a certain connection to Arbroath. I imagined a more charged atmosphere there for me. It was the place where my personal history pooled and collected, and the only place to go and do this.

We were quiet on the train. Looking out the window the sun kept flashing over the hills and stabbing at my eyes. I finally pulled the blind and asked Calandra, "What will you do next?" I tried to sound pleasant.

"Return to Glasgow, I guess," she said, "It would be nice to connect with family again, particularly my nephews."

She seemed tired and sad, and it occurred to me she hadn't slept well, while I slept like the dead, as always. I cracked a joke about this but she took it seriously, saying, "There's nothing wrong with being rested when you go to meet your fate. I'm actually a little envious." And with a tight smile on her face she folded her hands together and stared ahead down the aisle of the train.

In the cemetery we knew to look for three angels on an impressive stone base and pry open a tightly fitted but ultimately loose panel at the back. I'd crawl in to find a pocket of still time, or so I'd been told. We held each other but it was an immensely hard thing to say farewell, and I don't think either one of us could've endured a long goodbye. There were one or two tears on her face when I stepped back, and she was smiling the same tight, weathered smile. Unable to think of anything to say, I bent to crawl into the space. Placing my hands carefully on the soft mud, I heard her say, "I never expected you'd crawl your way into time travel like you're back on the playground." I laughed, loudly enough that I'm sure she heard. Maybe she was already turning to leave and maybe she wasn't. Inside, I saw the entire stone base was hollow and there was room to sit with my legs crossed. I held still. I was conscious it was a dark, tight space with a heavy smell of earth as I lifted the panel back into place. I was sure I'd disturbed some leaves when crawling inside. Not knowing what to wait for, I tried to breathe deeply to remain calm and still, but like falling asleep, I was gone before I knew it.

36: Tomas

As your plane lands and you wait through the discomfort of changes in air pressure, you don't suddenly decide to share that you're going to revive your father with the middle-aged woman next to you—possibly by digging him from a tomb if your information is correct—so you can finally get to know him. In any case, the woman spent most of the flight sighing and rattling her large frame in the small amount of space available to her and occasionally mumbling, "Never again." When she asked if I'd slept I thought for a moment she felt genuine concern, but it was a set-up for the complaint, "I wish I could." I suppose I could have said, "At the age of twenty I'll finally meet the father I don't know," but it would only have meant more questions and I preferred to hang onto what silence I could gather.

I took a train to Arbroath and a cab to the cemetery, tempted to hang my head out the window like a dog to avoid the unfolding smoke of the driver's cigarette. Grateful to be free of the cab, I stood in the sunlight a moment before casually searching around tombstones and tufts of yellowed, overgrown grass to find my future. I knew to look for three angels on a large, stone base. After ten minutes I found it and it was a simple matter to examine a panel on the back away from the path and pry it loose, finding it to be neatly fitted but not otherwise secured.

The sunlight spilled into the opening. My father sat there, one crisp leaf like a little tiger claw suspended just above the ground, very close to his foot. He was unnaturally still, like a life-sized photo of the man I never got to know, the stillborn father. I reached for him and he began. It was as simple as releasing a pendulum to allow it to swing once more. It's an unconscious, automatic part of the senses that confirms someone is breathing and has a heartbeat. Trying to use it purposefully was like employing a weak muscle but I could tell he was alive as I took him by the shoulders and pulled him free. He lay upside down to me, squinting and blinking at me in the sun.

"That was fast," he said, and I recognized no time at all had passed for him. I liked him for his calm. As he slowly stood and dusted himself off, he arrived at a statement, obvious but warmly put: "It's you." I'd expected him to be groggy or tired the way I'd been by the end of my flight, but there was none of that, and of course it had been the wrong instinct to expect it in the first place. "It's Tomas," I said, and he smiled a slow, full smile and embraced me, which is the kind of moment that takes any possible resentment away as surely as a strong wind takes a hat.

Before we could speak again, we felt something indescribable stir around us. I can only say we felt our bodies become alert as though the earth shifted when nothing had moved. Later we'd determine that lying frozen through so many years would displace a certain amount of time, as though his body had been a stick in a river. We saw flashes of movement, mourners who moved in a flurry of black clothing across the landscape like a murder of crows, a dark blur of activity with small, bright smears of flowers. We were bumped aside by anguish, and brushed in different directions by other events, now rushing through the terrain. One black hearse after another fast-forwarded to a halt and ejected a coffin like a torpedo. Thin cyclists followed the same road and dashed along the billowing stream of mourners like pilot fish.

"Get somewhere safe!" Oliver yelled as he made his way over to lie beneath a bench as I pressed myself against a tree. We watched everything slowly settle as the fast-moving, ghostly images careened around us from our relatively safe positions. I laughed at the idea of one person after another, for decades, resting their collective asses over my father as time caught up and saw that Oliver was returning my stupid grin from his own place of safety. Nobody but a blissfully free child would suffer the indignity of crawling under a park bench during a funeral, and they were all tugged to funerals rather than given the opportunity to collide with an invisible spirit under the bench.

"This is insanity!" I yelled to my father, as though into the wind, but he was laughing, too. It would seem there are few trees safer than a cemetery tree. Not many joggers or mourners took the time to examine my spot. There were flashing movements of darkness and colour. I saw a businessman with a cigar looking around as though to check if anyone noticed him. I saw a young woman holding a book with long, dark hair that fell over her blue dress. She looked up at the immense tree, put a hand out to feel the bark and then brought her hand back. She closed her eyes a second and then she was gone. The world around us fell back to normal. Had she just been here? Maybe in the last year? I felt like I was a little in love as I glanced around before going to help my father up.

37: Penelope

"You can't do this," I told Blake when he appeared at my home. The sense that I was intrigued by Blake had long since been dismissed by his self-centred nature. He was among those men who'll bring a woman to a certain level and then leap after his own pleasure like an animal unable to resist the food in front of it. And now there were these sudden, intrusive appearances. I came to feel he shouldn't be in my life at all, but he persisted.

He was even in a dream of mine, both Oliver and Blake on a game show behind podiums demonstrating their knowledge about subjects as obscure as British television drama and the number of symphonies Beethoven completed. Oliver guessed ten symphonies but was told by an oily host, "Beethoven died working on the tenth, so he completed nine." There was more, though my memory of it is confused and faded, as often happens with dreams. Blake missed a question about when the First World War had started and Oliver was set to win when a question about archery came up. Blake knew the answer: "Archery declined with the invention of firearms, but enjoyed a revival in the eighteenth century when it became fashionable again."

But the game wasn't resolved. Instead, the host slowly fell away from the conversation and they turned to each other. Blake was always arrogant, and while it was tempting to dislike him for this alone, he did have intelligence and a slim handsomeness that helped to balance the haughtiness to a degree. He stood in his dark blazer: "If you neglect your woman, you open up an opportunity for any old Blake. We're talking here about a man who left for twenty years to tumble through the world. Twenty years, for crying out loud."

But he seemed false, angry and poised at the same time. He showed that the personality he demonstrated to the world was as neatly arranged as his jackets and shirts were. This is finally the instinct that kept me from him, subtle enough that it was clarified to me in a dream: he wasn't genuine enough. Oliver should know he was lucky. It wasn't that I refused to move on and never would have considered someone else; above all, falseness troubled me and above all Oliver was a plainly charming man, comfortable in his own skin and with nothing to prove.

And then he was back, framed in our doorway as the breeze behind him ransacked the tree in our yard. Tomas came in first but wisely moved aside. "Mother," he said. "Father has returned, tired from twenty years of struggle to reach us again. He has held us in his heart all this time."

Oliver stepped in. For a few seconds my eyes couldn't take him in. Of course, that's our somewhat romantic way of saying it, when really my mind couldn't handle the sight of him: his same short hair, his round and handsome face. For a moment I thought he looked much older. I thought he had wrinkles, his head utterly robbed of its dark hair, his eyes dimmed. I couldn't believe it was Oliver. In my confusion, I stepped back. He took another soft step forward and I saw it was a trick of shadows and light. Oliver was older, but recognizably the same and not an old man as I had thought. A small river of bitterness in me threatened to swell and overflow but was quickly washed aside when the warmth in his eyes opened a floodgate of the same in me.

"I'm hungry," he said. We stood and talked in the doorway for long minutes before we even thought to move away to sit, so precious was our time. It was gradually less jarring to see him, less of a miracle every moment, beginning with opening a can of soup for him. It's true that we'll never forget the reunion and the feeling that came with it. We can think of it like an island above the placid surface of our daily experience: the moment we were utterly astonished with the existence of the other.

38: Blake

I HAD FOLLOWED MY PENELOPE. I DROVE THE PLEAS-
ant, tree-lined corridor of her street over and over again. I
slowed to see him return to stand on the front steps of the
house. I was transfixed, watching him step so undeserv-
edly inside. Her hands hesitated in the air but then found
places on his broad back. His son was there, too, and the
three of them didn't take the slightest notice of me before
I peeled away.

So I began my secret war. I'm not a stalker. Those people
don't have the slightest understanding of what's best for
their loved ones. I have an awareness of injustice stronger
than most. Sometimes I picture a map of the world shaded
to different degrees like a heat map, except it shows where
there were greater or lower levels of injustice. And while
some injustice like, say, a holocaust are easy to pick out,
many others are much quieter and form the subtle base
from which the rest of it springs. Only a small few of us,
elected by our sensitivity and education, can attempt to
change the world.

If I had to be honest, I'd have to say I'd always considered women to be one kind of prize or another. Few have *astounded* me. Relationships were always like classes to me; you learn something from them and move on, but you don't stay in the same class for decades because what would be the point? I would walk the streets trolling for women just to let them go a few months later. Penelope changed all that. When she wasn't around I felt anxious. I walked the streets feeling I'd forgotten something important, like I'd left the tap running in my apartment. I'd disconnected the doorbell long ago after one woman rang it repeatedly to get me to come down. For years I've just said it was broken and told people to call me when they arrive, but now I worried Penelope would visit and I wouldn't know.

I waited in the parking lot at her workplace and pretended to emerge from my car just in time to run into her, but I sensed she was aware I'd made some kind of special effort. She was polite but distant. More importantly, she declined to see me soon. Days passed. I sent a friendly note expecting an immediate reply and refreshed and refreshed my screen, but it simply blinked back at me, resetting in the same plain and agonizing manner. It seemed appropriate to send another message about the injustice, the inappropriateness of taking back a man destined only to hurt her again, an undeserving man. I explained that for the first time I felt I could be a deserving man. And then a brief reply, at last arriving in my inbox like a colourful little bird. It declared she didn't feel I was the right thing for her, along with a few more words wishing me well.

Wishing me well, a wishing well. It was as though the one wish I had was a hard coin in my pocket and I couldn't spend it. Calling her only went to voicemail, and she changed her job, so there was little point trying to find her there. I drove by her house for a year and it frequently yielded very little until I finally caught sight of him, the husband who would now enjoy the nightly comfort of her bed once again. My thoughts became more dramatic, concentrated and angry. I'm not accustomed to losing, particularly when the cost is high. My thinking turned to Oliver. I saw him at least as frequently as I saw her; it was as though the world kept offering him to me somehow, and I slowly came to recognize he was an obstacle that could be removed.

I invested in a second used car to allow for different appearances and circled the block or walked around Oliver's house. Unable to look directly at it, I came to know its sounds and rhythms. For example, Oliver usually left at around eleven in the morning through the back door. He was no doubt meeting people, informing friends he was back and starting work on the network of contacts he'd previously dropped. From the back door he walked behind an old garage and down a dirt path through a handful of trees that took him to another street and finally the subway.

On a quiet night at four in the morning I walked to the house, casually glanced at the back door and carried on to the garage. I put my hand delicately on the peeling white paint as I stood behind it. Here I would make my stand, and change the world for the better. By eleven in the morning I was tired and brittle with nervous energy, but excited. I became even more excited at hearing the familiar creak of the door. I waited. When Oliver appeared, it was only to start out again down the path, but I caught up with him, clumsily putting one hand over his mouth and with the other, driving a knife into his back. He let out a muffled cry and to my surprise, kicked out with a foot, making contact with a tree and sending us both backwards.

We fell and fell. It was the most extraordinary feeling to expect to hit the ground and instead find oneself in freefall. The trees rushed away and a translucent, overlapping haze of colour and movement closed in on either side of my vision like curtains. It was suffocating for a moment, and I held my breath as though underwater.

39: Athena

"You were always a lucky one, Oliver," I once told him. Not all the time. Not every moment of every day. I can name at least one thing that went wrong: I'd sent a much earlier message back to Penelope about how Oliver was available to them in the cemetery where Tomas eventually found him. Penelope would've lost Oliver and learned almost immediately he was waiting for her. But the message was gone, a minnow in a tremendous waterfall of events.

I checked the data, surprised at the number of years that had ticked by, and sent another message to Tomas: "I can help you find the father you don't know but deserve to know." Tomas brought him home. As a result, Oliver met the man he hadn't raised; and yet, even after that, events conspired to give Oliver another chance. He was not the brightest or the strongest of men, but he was blessed with second chances, surrounding him like a bed of leaves. Another chance to defeat an opponent, another chance to get home.

Blake stabbed Oliver and they fell together like drunks. I'd never have anticipated this, but they fell through time and Oliver had the advantage of recognizing it first. Blake withdrew the knife and the energy Oliver owned moved to heal the wound, working to return that small part of him to the way it was. Time became soft around the wound, the knife, the hand, and finally the two of them, so that they were both lost.

They fell together, grappling and suffocating through the heat of events for long minutes. There were no words spoken. Oliver saw what was happening and pulled them in a particular direction, but Blake was no fool. He must have read about time travel to at least some extent because he caught site of a few signs of his own personal geography and pulled them in that direction, thinking vaguely of his own personal timeline.

In the confusion, Blake struck Oliver again with his knife and would have stabbed him in the heart, but I arranged for him to miss, slipping a pillow of air and time between his arm and Oliver, even taking the extra step of loosening his fingers and pulling the knife from them. As Oliver reeled, he was able to see clear of the skyscrapers and cigar smoke, pulling them free like two languid swimmers. Through a long distance of falling boulders and hurrying trains, he pulled them in the direction of his son's birth.

Blake, however, had caught sight of Penelope. It was only her distant childhood burning like a star, but as he reached for it he saw her childhood home like an old movie, brief flashes of distorted colour blending together. Someone kicked fall leaves, then soundless children moved toward a birthday cake. Blake was a quick learner. He reached further in the direction of that hidden, remarkable time with the idea of becoming her childhood friend. Finally furious, Oliver stuck back, hitting Blake across the face. As the two of them grappled and spun together, Oliver held tight and twisted his weight, throwing Blake further back than he'd intended until Blake was lost before the brief trail of their lives even began. Free to swim and struggle the way he wanted, Oliver searched for the moment he wanted most, the time after his son was born, when he'd left his family.

And that was the end of his travels. I said a quiet farewell to my friend, in the hope of seeing him in the world at a less worrying time. I felt I'd see him again some cold, bright day. Oliver began again where he left, which made him a very lucky man, indeed. I like to think a particular kind of happiness isn't more than a man deserves if he's also given the opportunity to be a better man. I stuck around for a bit and saw Oliver learn the mixture of love and pressure that came with new fatherhood; to learn of the rewards and begin to gather up an idea of whom his son would become.

"He stops crying!" Oliver said, learning that when he sang to his son—only a small bundle in his arms—Tomas stopped fussing and looked up at him, his eyes wider. He knew those small eyes would grow up to drink in paintings and oceans. He knew that he now woke to a certain pressure, difficulty breathing. "It's like someone put a stack of plates on my chest," he told Penelope. But it slowly got better, as he saw they were managing. His own childhood lay as wetlands, somewhere deep in the bottom of his mind, faintly allowing comparisons to the experience he gave his son.

40: Oliver

Now I understand. I've looked down into the calm and uncomprehending eyes of my son at twenty months old and I've been struck with the idea that you lose everything you love. Even if nothing were ever to remove him from me, he'll grow and this child will be gone. The way they change teaches you that, and it teaches you to appreciate the moment. On some level parents are willing to have a second child at least partly to start over and begin again at the first step. But there isn't any way to cheat time. You can only begin a new process. Time is relentless. Time notices us and stares. In a similar way, water noticed the *Titanic* and kept staring until it covered every corner of the great ship. In this world, shy people are stamped out because we have no patience for their awkwardness, but underneath our impatience is the fact that they live their lives owning secret knowledge we'd rather ignore, like that it's unlucky to be noticed.

All I'd known when Tomas was coming was that I felt the gates of my old life closing. Fatherhood felt like a trap.

I hadn't thought about how I would live on in my son. I thought only about the sacrifice, the most superficial kind of lost freedom, without thinking of my new freedom to grow. When he was twenty months old I went into his room to look down in his crib, and as my eyes adjusted I found him among all his stuffed toys, arms folded to form a small arc, an arrowhead of potential. All around I sensed the parts of the world that were indifferent to him: a river of cars outside, pushing a space someone can be killed in, the electricity curled in the walls wanting to stop his heart, the angry people who'd thrash him. More than anything, I wanted to protect him.

On my permanent return to the time I'd left, I became something of a celebrity. Nobody had ever stepped back and reappeared moments later looking the same and capable of telling their story. I wrote down names: Maddy and Aldman, Fernando and Victoria. I made note of them all and told their stories, though I had little evidence of anything. They became like an old film I remembered watching, and while I remembered it warmly, the details began to escape me.

I was a distracted celebrity, sitting on an interview couch and pausing in the middle of a reply to see the parts of the camera unassembled, the bolts pulled into the air and melted back into the earth, the cameraman as a plump, bullied child surrounded by a halo of summer. The side effects lasted only a few months, but it was enough, thankfully, to sabotage media interest in following me around for various comments and statements. Even later, I'd stare off into the distance when they asked me something and I'd think of Penelope. It was an amusing way to thwart their efforts.

"Check this out," Penelope said, and we laughed at changing a diaper and finding a pea in his belly button. I was proud that my son lived in love, shrugging off kisses like rain. I was reminded of the moment I knew I loved Penelope. We sat in a café and I read about the 1971 atomic bomb test on Amchitka Island, uninhabited but for an entire sea otter colony. So many people don't think of anything but themselves, but later Penelope said, "I keep seeing hundreds of sea otter heads, all turning at once."

I knew nothing except that I wanted to protect her and Tomas, and that compassion was an essential ingredient in the world. It isn't much of a starting place, but everything starts somewhere. I'm not a great artist with a painting that will hang in a gallery for a century or two. I'm not a politician skilled and fortunate enough to have a career that ends in a prominent statue. My story is the story of a common man. I will extend a hand into the future and be remembered for some small distance through a child who'll think of me in so many different moments. Often enough they'll reflect on each other and together make the image of a man. A teacher might accomplish something similar with a reflection in the minds of her students. To live is to burn away in one place or another, and when a sun dies, its light strikes elsewhere for a time. This is to be remembered, until the last light falls.

Acknowledgements

MY THANKS TO SILAS WHITE, NATHANIEL MOORE and everyone at Nightwood Editions, including Amber McMillan for the careful edit of the book.

I'm grateful to my friends, in particular Pino Coluccio, for their unfailing interest in seeing this book published. Thanks also to my entire family for their support. To Elizabeth and our children: becoming a father has helped infuse this book with meaning I didn't know it would have at the start: thank you.

Thank you to the Ontario Arts Council for the financial support through the Writers' Reserve program.

PHOTO CREDIT: DEREK WUENSCHIRS

About the Author

ALEX BOYD WRITES POEMS, FICTION, REVIEWS AND essays, which have appeared in many publications such as *The Globe and Mail* and *Taddle Creek*. He helped establish *Best Canadian Essays*, co-editing the first two collections of work selected from Canadian magazines. Boyd's poetry collections include *Making Bones Walk* (2007), winner of the Gerald Lampert Award for best first book of poems in Canada, and more recently *The Least Important Man* (2012). He lives in Toronto.

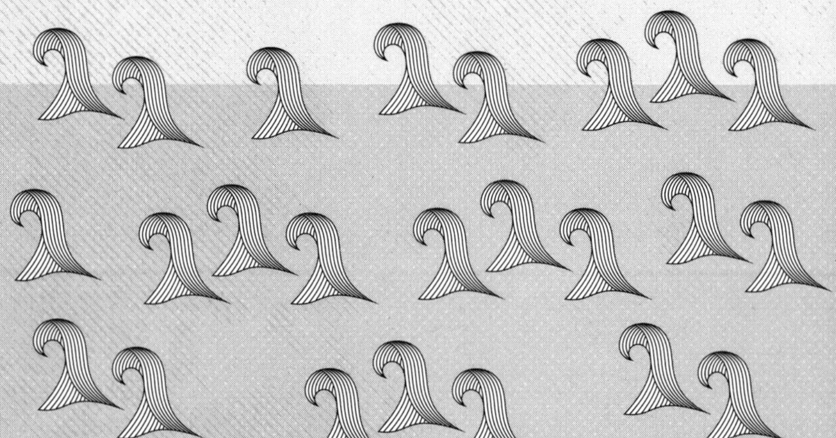